Checking on the House

Linda Hudson Hoagland

DEDICATION:

To the loves of my life:

MICHAEL E. HUDSON

MATTHEW A. HUDSON

ACKNOWLEDGEMENTS

"Four Large Eggs" - 2009 - Published as "A Lift Up – Not a Hand Out" in <u>A Cup of Comfort for a Better World</u>

"Life's Little Surprises" - 2006 - Published in NEWN

"What Choice Did She Have?" – 2009 – Published in Clinch Mountain Review

Publish America (America Star) of Baltimore, Maryland, for originally publishing this
novel in 2011.

Victoria Fletcher, fellow author, for editing and formatting this book. She also developed the cover design for the book.

CHAPTER 1
WHY ME?

"Remember, Sonny, I'll be back here first thing tomorrow. I'm just going to go home, check on the critters, straighten the house a bit, and take the mail in along with the newspapers. Then I'll be back. You won't be here alone very long. I love you so just hang in there and I'll be right back."

"I'll be fine, Honey. You go ahead," said the man who was attached to a heart monitor, a catheter, and several IV's.

I didn't want to leave but I knew I had to. It was time to go home and check on the well-being of everything that we had been working for all of our married lives. It wasn't much. It was the Stillwell County Habitat House. The first one they built in the county, but it was ours and I wanted to make sure it was still standing. I wanted to make sure the contents, as meager as they were, were still there.

Also, Sonny's little dog, Fred, was all alone. My son checked on him periodically, but he was alone for long periods of time. I take that back. Fred was sharing the house with three cats. One was a kitten who was aggravating the fire out of poor old Fred. I needed to go check on the food and the water and the mail and the newspapers and everything that involved everyday living even though we weren't living there at the moment.

Sonny was in the hospital in Roanoke again with those never ending heart problems. This had to be about the seventh or eighth time in the last six months, that he had been in Roanoke with heart problems. Each time he went, I

5

worried about whether or not he would leave those halls of healing again. Each time they pulled him from the edge of death in the emergency room, I worried about whether it was the right decision or not. He was fifty-nine and he was too young to die and I wasn't ready to lose him.

I walked slowly to the car thinking about everything that had been happening. My mind wasn't on the task at hand except for the fact that my feet were moving. I was bound and determined to get through this hospital visit with my husband alive.

The parking garage seemed like miles away when I started the long walk. The path I followed was all enclosed areas that tunneled under the ground. I was not exposed to outside elements until I was in the parking garage itself. That I knew. I had been sleeping in my car.

I didn't have the money, the forty-five dollar a night fee, to stay in the motel that had an agreement with the hospital to only charge that amount which, in their opinion, was a small amount. We had already been there five days. That would have so far required four nights stay in a motel and that was two hundred dollars I didn't have. I just barely had enough money to buy food and to drive back and forth which was a darn sight cheaper than staying in a motel; especially when it was day to day and I never knew when he was going to be released to go home.

My car and I had become very good friends. I would go out to the passenger side of the car as soon as visiting hours were over where I would make myself comfortable. I would work on maybe my writing or, if I had enough light, I would read a bit. Then I would just go to sleep.

There wasn't anything else to do except maybe watch the drunks totter in and out. There weren't many of those. Actually it only happened on one night when two tipsy young ladies decided they were going to cause a disturbance on the fifth level of the parking garage forcing the hospital police to show up and try to calm them down. I never did know what the disturbance was about but there was so much laughter and frivolity going on that I knew it wasn't anything important.

I actually slept better in my car than I did in the waiting room on the hard benches, if I could find one, with the lights shining brightly all night long. At least, in my car I could get semi-comfortable by pushing back the seat, tilting the back of it far enough until it was almost flat against the seat behind me. I grabbed a pillow and blanket and got down to the work of sleeping.

Most of the time there was absolutely no activity in the parking garage except for people going to the hospital, either employees or family members of people who were hurt. Possibly there was someone who had dropped a person off at the emergency room who had come to find a place to park before they could return to the person they had dropped off.

It never occurred to me that there was anything unusual about sleeping in my car in the parking garage. I had no reason to believe anything otherwise. I had been sleeping in it so it is my home, too.

I backed the car out of my space slowly, turned on my radio for the weather forecast, and I just had one of those feelings. I couldn't explain it. It was just there. It was like déjà vu all over again. I didn't know. It was just a feeling that something wasn't quite right.

I had my cell phone and I called into the hospital before I continued on my trip.

I talked to the nurses at the ICU nurses' station asking them how my husband was.

"Oh, he fine, Mrs. Holcombe. He's doing well. He has fallen asleep. We gave him a shot for pain."

"Well, thank you. I have to leave town. I will be back in the morning. You have my cell phone numbers. If you need me, you can get me there."

"That's fine, Mrs. Holcombe. There should be no problem at all. Everything is under control here. We will watch him closely."

Well, that wasn't the problem.

Now, I guessed maybe I better look at all of the lights on the car. No – no idiot lights showing me that anything was low of fluid or fuel or broken. Didn't feel any tire pressures uneven. Didn't hear any foreign sounds that shouldn't be pinging and banging and booming. So, I guessed it would pass. Maybe it was unrelated to this trip whatsoever. Maybe the feeling was just about my son in Virginia at home in his little house in Baptist Valley. Or maybe it was a bad feeling about my other son in Nebraska. But whatever the reason, something was wrong.

The drive from Roanoke to Stillwell was approximately two to two and a half hours long; two if you could drive five miles above the speed limit the entire distance which I had not been able to do or two and a half hours if you observed the traffic movement and the speed limit all the way there. Actually, one time it took me over three hours because of the repair work that was being done on one of the roads that had the traffic backed up for miles and I was in that back up.

It was a boring drive and I was not a radio listener. I got out of that habit years earlier. It bothered me. My husband used to turn it on full blast and you couldn't say two words. So I had gotten to where I wanted it off and I kept it off. I couldn't talk unless I had it off.

He honored my request and he always had it turned off when I was in the car. I was sure it was blaring when I wasn't there but I didn't care.

He loved his music. I used to. Music usually inspired memories that I was not ready or prepared for to be visualized again and again. It wasn't that all of my memories were bad. As a matter of fact, they weren't. I just didn't want to relive that part of my life over and over again. It was because I always associated music with people, certain people I loved very much or ended up hating very deeply.

So, I would sometimes start conversations with myself to keep myself alert or slap myself in the face so that the pain would keep me awake. That sounded stupid, but it worked. If it was a chilly day outside, I would roll the window down and the cool air blowing against my face helped keep me awake.

Sleeping in the car tended to make me tired most of the time. Sleeping in a hospital, anywhere in that hospital, tended to make me tired. I was looking forward to a night's rest in my bed. The only obstacle was getting there.

"I must be getting a flat tire. I hear a thump. I wonder what that is. I hear it again."

Now I was talking to myself big time.

"Was that somebody saying something?"

I rolled my window up quickly but I didn't hear anything again.

I rolled the window back down so I could keep the cool refreshing air in my face.

"Oh well, must have been my imagination. Maybe it was something on the road."

I kept driving.

The area I was driving through was isolated. The only signs of activity were traffic, mine and anybody who was in front of me or behind me. I was looking back in my rearview mirror to see if I was alone on this deserted stretch of highway.

Well, I was alone and it was late.

"Why in the world did I decide to leave so late?" I wondered. "God knows how much I hate driving at night."

Just the thought of getting it done for some reason was upper most in my mind. I had to do it.

"Keep driving, Ellen. Keep driving," I admonished myself. "I see no – wait a minute – there is a set of lights.

It's coming towards me on the other side of the four lanes. I'm not alone out here, thank God."

Suddenly I heard a crash, a huge crash- bang, boom- coming from the back of my car.

"What the heck was that?"

I quickly slowed my speed and got off on the side of the road. I was afraid to look. What if my car was falling apart at this time of night? I had no money. I couldn't even get the thing towed to get it fixed.

I jumped out of the safe cocoon of my car into the overwhelming darkness. I reached back into the car for the flashlight that I had in the glove compartment. I walked around the vehicle to see if the tires were all intact. I bent down and couldn't see anything dragging underneath. I didn't think it was that kind of noise. It didn't sound like that kind of noise at all.

I walked around the car again and I heard a tap coming from the back of the car. I reached inside the car and hit the button that opened the trunk.

Out popped a man.

"Oh my God. Where did you come from?"

"All right, Lady," said the man as he was trying to straighten up after being folded into that trunk for God knows how long.

"What do you want?" I asked.

"I want to ride in your car upright sitting in the seat next to you while you drive me."

"I can't. I'm on my way home. My husband is seriously ill."

"You will do what I say," he said as he pulled a gun from behind his back.

"Well, I guess I will," I said as I stare wide-eyed at the gun that seemed to grow in size as I gazed at it.

I looked at him, my eyes wide with fright. *Why in the world is this happening to me? Don't I have enough problems with a seriously ill husband?*

"I was always told that God would only give you the problems you could bear. My shoulders are sagging, God. I can't bear very much more," I said as I started to cry.

"Don't cry, Lady. Be quiet."

"That's easier said than done. What do you want?" I asked between sobs.

"I want a ride. That's all I want. Now you stand over here while I take a leak."

"You're kidding me, aren't you?"

"No, that's why I had to get out of that trunk. I need to take a leak. Now go over there and stand while I hold this gun on you. If you make one move, I'll shoot you. I'll blow a hole clean through you."

"Okay, okay, no problem. I'll do what you say," I whispered as I held my hands up.

"Put your hands down, Lady, I don't want people to think there is something wrong here as they go by."

"Okay," I said as I dropped my hands to my side.

Obviously there might be something wrong, but a passerby in the middle of night would definitely not stop to check it out. At least, I wouldn't have stopped since I was a lone female in a car.

Some strong, masculine, macho male might do it. So, I guessed he was right. I had to put my hands down.

"All right, Lady, let's get in the car. Do you have a cell phone on you?"

I didn't know what to say. I didn't want to tell him I did. I didn't want to tell him I didn't. I could only hope he didn't hear me call the hospital when I first climbed into the car while he was ensconced in the trunk. I didn't want to give up my cell phone to him. I might need it. But, what if it rang while I was sitting there next to him in that car? It was in my pocket and while I was in the hospital I had set it on vibrate. After I called the nurses, checking on Sonny, I wondered if I had kept it on vibrate. I didn't remember changing it to ring but I might have. Just an automatic thing. It was in my pocket and I was going to leave it there. I was not going to tell him. It was one of those little tiny fold up flat ones that you really couldn't detect. Being the short chubby female that I was, I didn't think he was going to search me.

"No – I don't have one. I can't afford one."

"What do you mean you can't afford one? They don't cost much, Lady."

"I have a husband in the hospital. He's eating up every bit of my funds. I'm barely able to pay for his prescriptions and the utilities at the house. I'm going through a debt solution group trying to get my credit cards paid off. I don't think that's working either. I get an awful lot of collection calls. I'm probably going to have to file for bankruptcy which is exactly what I didn't want to do. So, I really don't have the money for any extras and I don't have any money to give to you. Maybe a couple of dollars. I was on my way home to see if I could borrow some."

"I don't want to hear your sob story, Lady. I've got problems of my own."

"Yeah, I bet you do."

The trunk lid was still open. Before he closed it, he reached inside and pulled out a duffle bag. I didn't know what was in that duffle bag and I was really afraid to find out. I thought finding that answer might cost me my life. I didn't pay any attention to his duffle bag.

He forced me around to the driver side of the car and while I crawled in, he held the gun directly on me. He pointed it at me at all times. He walked around the front of the car, then to the passenger side where he climbed inside the vehicle himself. All the time, he was holding that gun steady on me.

I would like to take the opportunity to start the car, step on the gas, and just run over him. I couldn't take the chance. I was afraid his trigger finger would be faster than my car. I let the moment pass. I didn't run him over like I wanted to do.

"Okay, Lady, drive."

Well, I didn't have any choice as to which direction to go. There was only one direction to go because I was on a freeway and the only way to go was whichever way the traffic was pointing at the time.

"Where to?"

"Just drive, Lady, that's all. Just drive and observe all of the speed limits. Don't go too slow – don't go too fast. Just go. Don't be weaving back and forth. Don't be giving no cop a reason to stop you."

"Okay, no problem. You can watch. See. I'm not doing anything wrong," I said as I pulled out into the empty stretch of road. The only traffic I could see was on the other side of the four lanes that were separated by a large median. There was absolutely no way to signal anybody for help.

The silence was making me nervous. When I got nervous, I chattered on and on.

"Are you running from the cops?"

"Why do you ask that?"

"You have a gun in your hand."

"Let's put it this way, I wouldn't be happy if a cop stopped me for any reason whatsoever. So that means if I'm not happy you're definitely not going to be happy. So don't let a cop stop us."

"Okay, what if it's something I can't help?"

"You'll be the one that's in trouble. I may be the one that they're after, but you'll be the one that dies."

"Okay, all right, where did you want me to drive you to?"

"Just keep driving. I'll let you know."

"I live in Stillwell, Mister. That's as far as I am going to go. That's about a hundred miles from here. Once I get there, I want to go to bed, get some sleep, get up, check on things at the house, and come back to Roanoke. Like I said, my husband is very sick. I do have to get back."

"Sorry, Lady. You'll do what I tell you to do and nothing else."

"Are we going further than Stillwell?"

"I don't even know where Stillwell is."

"The other side of Bluefield, West Virginia."

"I don't know. We'll see."

"My name is Ellen. What's yours?"

"That's cute, Lady. Do you really think I'm going to tell you my name?"

"Well, no, maybe not. What if I call you John?"

"Why?"

"Well, it's better than Hey Stick-Up Man, Hey Robber, Hey Killer."

"All right, all right, if that's what you want. Call me John, if that will make you happy."

"Are you from around here, John?"

"Where's here?"

"Well, right now it's a hundred miles from Stillwell."

"No, I'm not. Quit asking so many questions."

"Why?"

"I'm not ready to answer any questions from you, from the cops, from anybody."

"Who are you running way from?"

"Well, you're the one that told me it's the cops, Lady. You believe that, okay?"

"Okay."

"Keep driving and stop with all the yak."

I sat and thought as I drove about what I could possibly do to get out of this mess.

How did I get into it anyway?

How did he get into my car?

I must have left the door unlocked. I don't remember doing that but it could have happened. Then, all he had to do was press the button on the dashboard to get into the trunk to hide. Someone must have been chasing him.

Who is chasing him?

Of course, I hadn't heard anything on the radio or television because I hadn't had the opportunity to listen to the radio or watch television, news programs, or anything of that nature. My husband did tune in the westerns and any sports activities he could find. That's all I ever got to see. The world could have come to an end and I wouldn't have known about it unless it was broadcast on the western channel or during the baseball game, or interrupting the football game, or the car race, or anything like that.

Why my car?

Why me?

I wondered if he had been watching the parking lot knowing that I slept in my car. He could have been doing that. That was interesting. Oh well, now I had discovered another reason why it was dangerous to sleep in my car. I'd ignored all of the other ones. This one had come back to bite me.

"Hey, Mister, John."

"Lady, what is it you want now?"

"Why did you get into my car?"

"The passenger side rear door was unlocked. It was the only one I could open so that's the reason. Once I got inside your car, I realized I could get the trunk open by pressing the button on the dashboard which is what I did. I waited for you to come out."

"How did you know I would come out?"

"In most cases, people who are visiting the hospital don't stay there forever. The employees don't stay there forever. They do come out after a period of time."

"Had you seen my car before? Had you seen it the day before?"

"No, Ma'am, I just happened to run up on it and found it unlocked and I crawled inside. To keep from being seen, I opened the trunk and got inside, after I relocked the door so that no one would suspect that I was hiding anywhere near your car."

"Okay, that sounds reasonable. What is it you're running away from?"

"Shut up, Lady."

"Okay. We've gone about twenty miles now. How much further do you want me to take you?"

"Just keep driving, Lady."

"Okay. I'm really worried about my husband, you know. He's got a really bad heart. He is in there for congestive heart failure this time. He almost didn't make it."

"Like I said, Lady, I don't want to hear your sob story."

"Aw, come on, Mister, I'm worried about my husband. I need to pull over so I can call."

"That's why you need a cell phone, Lady."

"Well, if I had one you would have taken it from me."

"You're right there. We're not going to pull over. Maybe at the next rest stop but not until then."

"Mister, I need to know about my husband. He is very sick."

"You weren't going to go back until tomorrow so you don't need to know right now."

Suddenly we hit fog in the middle of the night on an unfamiliar road. That could be very scary. There were no cars in front of me with their taillights glaring so that I could follow them. I was forging my own path straight ahead and who knew what mountain I was going to go over because, right at that moment, we were climbing a mountain. As long as I stayed within the lines, if I could see the lines, I would be okay. I would drive slow enough to be a danger to anyone else coming up behind me but that was all right because they could pass me on the other side- if I knew where my side was.

The fog was thick and the headlights were reflecting. It was almost like standing in a vapor but I was driving a car at sixty-five miles an hour. I was not standing. I slowed down to about fifty.

"What are you doing, Lady?"

"I can't see anything. The fog is as thick as pea soup here."

"All right, it is hard to see but don't go any slower. You'll attract attention."

"What attention? There isn't anybody out here."

"I know but I don't want any reason for attention."

"I'll probably attract attention for driving too fast in this fog."

"Okay, Lady, if that's what you think."

I slowed it down to about forty and prayed that I wouldn't run off the road and over the side of the mountain.

Suddenly there was no fog. I had gone down the mountain far enough to have gone into the valley that hasn't quite filled up with the fog yet. It seemed to be lingering around the mountain tops.

"Okay, Lady, now you can pick up the speed."

I nodded at him and I pressed my foot to the floor.

"Not that fast, Lady. You know what I'm talking about."

"Okay. Where is it you have to be? At what time, John?"

"Just drive, Lady."

"Okay."

I was getting tired of saying okay but that seemed to be the only response I could muster up. Okay was the only thing left in my world. Everything was okay. It wasn't fine. It wasn't great. It wasn't wonderful. It was okay. We were still getting by. No matter what anybody said, we would muddle through.

Now, I began to wonder. I was worried about the death of my husband looming in the not too distant future. Now, I was going to have to worry about the death of myself from the gun pointing directly into my side.

What am I going to do?

How am I going to get out of this?

I didn't have a clue.

CHAPTER 2
PLEASE HELP ME!

"Hey, John."

"What is it now?"

"I have to go pee. I have to go pee really bad."

"How far are we from a rest stop?"

"I saw a sign back there. It should be within the next mile or so."

"That's awful convenient, isn't it, after you saw the sign?"

"Well, it could have been what planted the idea in my head. But I really can't help it. I'm an old lady and I have to go pee. Once the idea gets there, the urge doesn't quit. If I don't go soon, it will be too late."

"All right, all right, when we get to that rest stop I want you to go inside the ladies' bathroom. There shouldn't be anybody there at this time of night. Do your business and come right back out. If you don't, I'll come in and get you gun a-blazing."

"Okay, but you've got to give me a little time. Like I said, I am an old lady."

"All right, Lady. Ellen. Ellen, you said your name was Ellen, right?"

"Yeah, it's Ellen."

"Do as I tell you and you might live to see your old man again."

"Okay, John, okay."

I was getting a wee bit tired of this stuff. The stress, the worry of my husband, the worry about trying to get back to work, the worry of keeping the house going, and feeding the animals. I had no time for this. This had to stop.

I pulled the cell phone from my pocket. "No Service" was displayed on the useless thing. I had to control my desire to throw the tiny toy.

I walked further into the ladies' room and wrote on the stall with an eyebrow pencil that I had shoved down into my pocket earlier and forgotten about. It had fallen out of my handbag and when I picked it up I didn't take the time to stuff it back into the right place.

> HELP! MY LICENSE NUMBER IS YMS3304, I THINK. THE MAN IN THE CAR HAS A GUN – PLEASE HELP ME!
> ELLEN HOLCOMBE

That was what I scrawled all over the bathroom stall door. It was the best I could do. It was all I could do in the time that I had to do it. Maybe somebody would believe it. Maybe somebody would help me.

I did my duties and after writing the message on the wall inside the stall, I left the bathroom.

He stuck his head in the bathroom door and determined that everything was okay.

He didn't check inside the stall.

We walked out to the car and I started driving again. My eyes were heavy but not from wanting to go to sleep like you would normally think. My eyes were heavy from being open for so many hours concentrating so many hours on whether my husband was going to live or die. It wasn't a question of needing to go to sleep. It was a question of exhaustion. Sometimes you just couldn't help it.

We drove on another twenty miles. We were getting closer to my home and I still hadn't determined where he was going.

"John?"

"What?"

"We're getting close to where I live. I had a thought, John."

"What's that?"

"I could let you off in Bluefield, the City of Bluefield, in West Virginia. It's a big city. At least it's a big city compared to Stillwell."

"What about this big city?"

"Well, you could get lost there. You could blend in. You could become a West Virginian and blend in."

"Let me think about it."

"Please, I want to go home and get some rest and go back to Roanoke to check on my husband."

I was near tears and I knew if I started crying again, I wouldn't be able to drive and that wouldn't make him happy. I sniffed and took a deep breath to try to clear away the urge to cry.

"I said I'd think about it, Lady. Settle down and drive."

"Okay."

"How much further is it to this city that you're talking about?"

"Bluefield, West Virginia. It's about thirty-five or forty miles from here. Then I live about fifteen or twenty miles on past Bluefield. Is that where you want me to drop you?"

"I don't know. I said I'd think about it. Just don't know. How big is that city?"

"I don't know. It's big though. It's big enough to be called a city not a town. So it's got to be big. I think it's probably over fifty thousand."

"That's not big."

"It's big around here. Not like the small town I live in. I like that small town but it's so far away from all of the medical facilities that my husband needs. But, I don't have any choice. I can't afford to leave here. I've got a job. I've got to stay in that small town. That job supplies the health insurance. The health insurance is what has been keeping my husband alive. If I didn't have that health insurance, he would have been dead by now. Medicare wouldn't pay for all of the problems he has. I know that. They would have come up with some way for the doctors not to treat him. So I have to keep the insurance. I have to keep my job."

"You do have a few problems, don't you, Lady?"

"Yes, Sir, I surely do. You're not helping a bit."

"No, I guess I'm not. I'll think about that Bluefield thing."

"Okay," I said as I tried to straighten up my mind and concentrate on not crying. I didn't want to cry. God help me, but I didn't want to cry. I didn't want to get him stirred up.

I continued to drive and worry about what was next. My husband was near to dying but with a little help from the doctors – I should say with a lot of help from the doctors – he would survive once again. Sometimes I wondered if that was a good thing. He had to go through so much but I loved him and I still needed the companionship of a loving husband. I hoped I wasn't being selfish.

"We're getting pretty close to Bluefield. Have you made up your mind?"

"How many more miles is it?"

"About twenty."

"What do you think I should do?"

"I really don't know, Mister - John. I know what I would do. If I was afraid the police would catch me, I 'd get out and get lost in Bluefield."

"You said it's not a big town or a big city. How can you get lost in Bluefield?"

"All towns and cities have vagrants of some kind. They have street people. Be a street person."

"You're so sure about all of this, aren't you?"

"No, Mister, I just need to get home. I need to get some rest and I need to go back to my husband. He's sick. Remember?"

"Yeah, Lady, you're not going to let me forget. Okay, you can let me out in Bluefield. But I'll pick the place. We'll drive around for a while and I'll pick the place."

"That would be great. Are you going to let me go when you do that?"

"No, I think I'm going to keep you with me for a while. I would be afraid that you would call the police."

"If I promised not to call them, would you let me go home? Would you please let me go home?"

"Let me see your car registration."

"Why?"

"I just want to see it. I need to get some information off of it."

"Why?"

"Let me see the car registration – now!" he said harshly as he poked the gun into my ribs.

"It's in the glove compartment. Right there," I said as I tried to point to the glove box built into the dashboard of the car.

"I'll get it out of there but don't be making any stupid moves."

He must be getting tired of saying that. He must be getting nervous.

I wonder what he was running away from. I wonder who he was running away from. He wouldn't tell me.

"What's in that bag, Mister?"

"It's none of your concern."

"Okay," which was the word I was saying the most lately. It seemed that I was saying it over and over again.

"What did you do that made you need to run?"

"It's none of your concern."

"Well, if I'm going to be traveling with you like you seem to think I am, don't you think I ought to know something about you? About what happened? So I will know what to expect? Will it be necessary for me to run from the cops, too? I mean, what if something happened to you and you left. They found out that you had been traveling with me. Will I be pursued? And for what?"

"That's a likely scenario, Lady. That's likely to happen."

"Why? Why would that happen? What did you do?"

"I took some money."

"Okay. Where did you take that money from?"

"A bank. It's in that bag, right there, and I'm not going to give it back."

"Why did you take the money?"

"Why do people steal money? Think about it, Lady. Why do people steal money?"

"You needed money. Why did you need so much?"

"I didn't need so much. I just wanted to take enough to get the hell out of there and have a life of my own. I don't think I got enough though. There's only about thirty thousand dollars in there and that's not going to take me very far."

"Sure it will. It'll take you to one of those foreign countries where thirty thousand dollars can last a life time there. The cost of living is so much lower than we have."

"Yeah, that's true, Lady, but then they don't have things that we have. They don't have the luxuries in life. I like those luxuries."

"Where were you planning to go?"

"I don't think I'll be telling you that."

"What if they caught you and made you talk? What if you wanted to talk?"

"I can't do that. I can't do that. I can't tell you that."

"Okay. So you robbed a bank. Did anybody get hurt?"

"Yeah, I shot the security guard."

"Did you kill him?"

"I don't know. He was an old man. If I didn't kill him, the fright probably did."

"So what are you planning to do about all of this?"

"What do you want me to do, Lady, turn myself in? That would be stupid. I'd be executed for capital murder if that man dies. I don't want that. Do you want that? Would you want that?"

"No, but I didn't rob a bank."

"How are they going to know that? How are they going to know that you didn't drive the getaway car?"

"I never thought about that."

"You're with me, aren't you?"

"Yeah, but I'm not with you willingly."

"You're driving me all over the place. You're giving me advice. You're my good friend, Ellen."

"Okay. You can do a number on me. Is that what you're saying?"

"Sure. How else do you think I'm going to keep you driving that car?"

"I think you ought to give me a break."

"Why, Lady? Are you going to give me one?"

"Yeah, when you get out of the car in Bluefield, I'm not going to tell anybody who you are or what happened."

"No, I'm not going to get out of the car in Bluefield."

"You're not? I thought you had decided you were?"

"You're going to get out of the car in Bluefield. I'm going to drive away," he replied smugly.

"So you're going to steal my car."

"No, Lady, you're going to give it to me."

"I can't give you my car. I've got to go back to Roanoke. I've got to see my husband."

"I understand that. You'll just have to borrow one."

"Who from?"

"You have friends, don't you?"

"Would you loan somebody your car to go a hundred and fifty miles out of town?"

"Yeah, if it was somebody that had to go, especially a family member."

"I don't have any family in town. I have a son who has a car. He lives about ten miles from me. He has to have his car to go to work. He can't loan me a car. He has no spare."

"You've got friends."

"Yeah, I've got friends. But do they have cars to lend me? Cars are a big investment now a days. They cost almost as much as a house. I'm sure they wouldn't have spare cars to lend me."

"Well, it's an emergency. I'm sure someone would lend you a car or take you to Roanoke."

"Yeah, but then how do I get back? I will have a sick husband to bring home."

"Call that son of yours, tell him to come and get you."

"He works. If he doesn't work, he doesn't get paid. He has to work. He's barely making ends meet."

"I don't know, Lady, you're just going to have to do something," he said with a shrug of his shoulders for emphasis.

"Yeah, I figured that out all by myself."

"There's a sign that says Bluefield next five exits, see?"

"Yeah."

"Get off at the next exit that goes into town."

"Okay."

I swerved off the freeway and drove on down the exit ramp. I was going slower than I should have been driving. Of course, he noticed it and poked me in the ribs.

"Okay," I pushed down on the gas pedal too hard and I was going too fast. I got another poke in the ribs.

"You'd think you'd learn, Lady. Quit that."

"Okay, I'm sorry. Just nervous."

"What part of town are we in now?"

"Bluefield is a pretty big town. It stretches several miles. This is the end where you're most likely not to blend in. This area is where people know their neighbors and know who lives here or who has a right to be here. You don't belong here; therefore, you would not blend."

"Drive on then."

About midway through town was where the main business district was located and that was where I had hoped he wanted to get out of the car because that location was closest to the police station.

"Okay, Lady, keep going."

"Why? Don't you want out in this area?"

"No, this is where the police are likely to be patrolling the area, in the business district. Where is the slum section or the section that the poor people live in?"

"On up a little further. Up by the college."

"That's where we're going. What college are you talking about?"

"Bluefield State. That area is a little on the poor side. It's not because of anything other than the fact that the people are poor. It's a little dangerous. There are drugs, there are robberies, and there's prostitution in the area. So – a stranger would have no problem."

"Is that where you plan to drop me?"

"No, I was planning to drop you in town."

"Why?"

"Because it was the safest place for me."

"Oh, I see. You weren't thinking about me then, were you?"

"Not especially. I was thinking about me. I have to get out of here. I have to go home. I have to get some rest. I have to go back to Roanoke and you're not letting me do that."

27

"You sound like a broken record, Lady. I heard that little tale of woe over and over again and I'm tired of it."

I started to cry. I wanted to cry this time. I wanted him to know I was upset and scared.

"Stop it, Lady. No blubbering."

"I can't help it. I need to get out of here. I need to go home."

"Where are we now?"

"See that up there. Up that hill right there."

"Yeah."

"That's the college."

"We want to go up there, don't we?"

"Yeah, that would be good. You could blend in with the college students up there. You're young enough. No one would know the difference."

"Is it patrolled at night?"

"I don't know. I've not been there at night."

"You never went to college."

"Yeah, but I went to one in Virginia, not West Virginia. I'm sure it is patrolled. It's in the city. It would be done by one of those rent-a-cops, you know. Those people the college rents that really aren't willing to get into a shoot'em-up with anybody because they are not paid enough for that. I wouldn't blame them one single little bit."

"Okay, Lady, let's go – up there. I want you to drive around a bit."

"Okay," I said as I turned into the long driveway that passed several buildings that were snuggled up against the hillside. The layout was strange in that it started close to midway on the hill and ranged up and out like bird houses perched on the hillside.

West Virginia, in this area, was in the Appalachian Mountains and it was hillside or maybe the right word would be mountainside.

It wasn't a bad college. It was just perched. The buildings were hard to get to if you didn't know your way around, which I didn't.

"Turn down that way, Lady."

"Okay."

I saw nobody milling around. I saw no security. Nobody was there that could help me.

"Stop over there, Lady. See where it is dark over there. There are no lights. Turn your car lights off here and drive over there."

"Why? What are you going to do?"

"Just do what I tell you."

"You're blended in. It's dark. This is a dark car. With the lights off, they won't be able to see it very well. What are you going to do to me?"

"Just shut up and do what I told you."

"You're not going to let me go, are you?"

"Shut up, Lady, and drive."

I edged my way forward in the car. I wasn't sure what was on the other end of that little paved area because it was so dark but the lights would help me see, I hoped.

"Turn off the lights."

"I can't see where I'm going."

"I said turn them off."

I pushed the button in – no more lights.

"You want me to pull in or back in to this spot?"

"Turn around, Lady, and back in. I want the trunk buried in the darkness."

"Okay."

I turned as slowly as possible trying to prolong whatever it was he is planning to do.

"You got a problem, Lady? Get this car backed in there – now."

"Yes, Sir."

What is his next step? Kill me? I hoped he wasn't going to kill me but I wasn't sure.

"Okay, Lady, I want you to get out of the car right now. Walk around to the back of the car."

"Why?"

"Just do what I say. I'm getting tired of everything and that includes your questions. Just get around to the back of the car."

I crawled out slowly and lingered, "Do you want me to lock the door?"

"No."

I was asking more of the questions that he was tired of. I walked around to the back of the car. Basically, I had to feel my way because I didn't see very well at all. I didn't have good night vision anyway. When you were in your fifties, the vision tended to fade away on you even more just due to natural age.

"Okay, give me your keys."

I gave him the keys and he felt around and poked it into the trunk.

"Now, get in."

"You're going to lock me in here?"

"Yeah, I have to do some scouting. I want you in the trunk. Then I'm going to take a little rest in the front part of the car and I don't want you moving around. I don't want you where you can be seen. If you make a noise, I'll blow you away."

The look on his face told me he wasn't kidding. He was tired. I was sure he was hungry. He was going to take it out on me, if I wasn't careful.

Trying to get my legs, knees, and chubby body into the trunk of that car was not an easy task. It was also not going to be comfortable, but I had to do it.

I had a newer model car and I had heard that you were able to unlock the thing from the inside. I didn't know how to do that. It was something I didn't think I would ever have to know. I didn't have any little kids running around so I didn't need to learn that operation so that I could show them. Now, I was sorry. I wished I had already found out. I didn't know I would need the information to save my own life.

I crawled into the car and prayed that he wasn't going to kill me.

I was grateful that I had a midsize car but I wished I had a large car like a Cadillac, a Lincoln, something like that would have a huge trunk. This wasn't the case. I had a Cavalier, a Chevy, and it was midsize. It had a relatively small trunk. You could put a body in the trunk. I was that body, if I was folded carefully. So, I didn't have much wiggle space.

I wondered if there was a light inside so that I could see the trigger to pop open the trunk. Or, maybe mess with a wire or two if I could reach them or even find them. Or, around the lock, there should be some kind of a latch to let me out. It was a newer model car.

What am I going to do?

The lid closed and the darkness overwhelmed me.

The tight small space caused a vision of a casket to pop up in my head. It wasn't even velvet or satin lined.

It is just a car trunk, Ellen.

How am I going to get out of here?

I had to keep poking around, but I couldn't do it right then. I had to listen to see where he was.

I heard steps, barely heard steps, walk away after he told me, "Don't make a sound, Lady. Not one sound."

I didn't know where he was going, but he wasn't next to the car so I started poking and prodding. I hadn't heard him climb into the car so I thought I might be safe for a few minutes.

Suddenly there was a voice, "What are you doing in there? I told you not to make a sound."

"I was just moving a little bit," was my muffled response. "I've got a cramp in my leg and I've got to go to the bathroom."

"You and the bathroom, Lady, you're going every hour now."

"I'm an old lady, remember? Old ladies lose control when they get older. They can't help it. Old men do, too. You've got this to look forward to someday."

"Shut up, Lady," he whispered harshly at me.

Well, how am I going to know if he is gone? I thought he had walked away before but he was standing there listening for me to make a sound, which I did, as I poked around the lock with my finger. *Now what am I going to do? Just lay there and die? No, it's not in me. If I'm going to die, he's going to have to kill me.*

I was going to find a way out of this mess, even if I died trying. I wanted to get back to my home and my husband. If I had to go back in a velvet-lined box, that was fine. At least, they would know I tried. They will all know that I tried. *God will know that I tried.*

I can't figure out why God is doing this to me.

I laid in the car trunk as quietly as possible not moving a muscle. I tried to get my poor cramping legs and knees more comfortable. That wasn't going to happen but I kept trying to do it quietly.

How am I going to get out of this mess?

Of course, I was always told God didn't put anything on your shoulders that you couldn't bear. My shoulders were starting to sag a bit.

"I'm getting tired, God. I'm getting real tired."

Tears were starting to creep down my cheeks and I knew I couldn't have that. I couldn't just lay there and blubber. I had to get out of there. *Think about tomorrow. Think about what you're going to do tomorrow.*

Once you get out of here, what are you going to do? Where are you going to go? How are you going to get there?

He had my keys but he didn't have my phone. I still had my phone.

Can I get to it? I wiggled around and it was on the hip that I was laying on which meant it was buried under my body in a pocket. *How am I going to get my phone?*

I couldn't turn over. I could barely move. I could barely stretch my legs out and I had very little arm movement. If I could push my body up, I could get my phone out with my other arm. It was buried deep in my pocket.

Now what?

I did everything I could to move around inside the trunk- the deep, dark, dungeon, of a trunk.

I didn't have to worry about getting cold. I had worked up a good sweat trying to get myself turned around. But, I wasn't turning. I didn't have enough room. All I could do was tip myself back a little to try to get my cell phone out from under me. It was deep in my pocket where I thought it would be safe from his hands. It was also safe from mine.

Maybe if I wiggle around, unfasten my pants – well – they don't have a fastener – they are elastic. If only I could wiggle out of my pants.

Can you imagine – I hoped there was no kind of camera or anything watching me do this. This had to be a disgusting sight. This fat little old lady trying to wiggle out of her pants in the trunk of a car.

If it's not hysterically funny, it's got to be downright shameful.

What could I do?

I tried to pull down my pants. I tried inch by inch by inch to get them down on one side.

If I flopped like a fish, which wasn't likely, but I would try anyway, I could start inching them down the other side. If I flopped like a fish and he was in the car, he would feel the movement.

Is he in the car?

I don't hear a thing.

I hear no snoring.

I haven't heard the car door open and close.

Where is he?

He left me here to die in this trunk.

I wasn't afraid of dying really. I knew eventually someone would show up in this parking lot. If they did, I would get some help.

Where is he?

What can I do?

How do I get out of this mess?

I didn't know what was going on.

I didn't know what bank he robbed.

I didn't know why he wanted to get the money in that duffle bag.

Maybe he had a really strong need to get that money. Maybe he had a sick relative. Maybe he had to pay ransom money. Who knew?

All I knew was that I was lying in my own car trunk because he stole money.

I paused a few minutes from wiggling and flopping around. It was wearing me out. I couldn't hear anything. I would have to pause so I could hear any noises. All I could hear was my own breathing from the exertion of trying to do big moves in tiny spaces.

I have to get out of here somehow.

I heard a noise.

I heard a car.

Is that what that is- a car – a vehicle?

Where is he?

Can I make a noise?

Can I beat on the trunk of the car?

Can I scream for somebody to come and get me?

What can I do?

It was gone.

I heard the vehicle- the sound- moving away from me, not towards me.

I missed it.

I cried.

I hated it so bad.

I wanted to go home. I wanted to go back to Roanoke.

"God, like I said before, I'm getting tired."

The next moment I was asleep. I slept an exhausted, frightening, sleep.

I was dreaming.

CHAPTER 3
I FROZE...

I was a child again, a teenager, perhaps a student just entering high school...

The dew covered the tall grass and weeds frightening my world with an unknown wetness that only I could feel. The darkness allowed me to see nothing.

I froze, crouched close to the wall; there was something out there – I had definitely heard it move in the blackness.

Then nothing – I heard nothing.

I crawled up from my crouch and continued walking.

The tree limbs swayed in the slight breeze casting eerie shadows on the deserted stretch of roadway next to the Clinch River. The long black fingers of darkness, silhouettes of the branches, reached across the gravel drive as if waiting to ensnare a victim in their long boney grasp.

For me, sixteen-year old Ellen Hutchins, the reflections cast by the full moon against a black sky seemed like a macabre omen on this Halloween night.

I had traveled the pathway hundreds of times during the evening hours to visit friends and family. Tonight, however, was different. I could feel it in the gentle breeze as it rustled in the dry, brightly colored leaves, in the absence of sound from the tree frogs and hoot owls, and in the blanket of fog rising from the riverbed like a smothering, low-flying cloud.

As chill bumps crept down my spine, I tried to rationalize my fear. Instead, I blamed it on an overactive imagination.

"I've seen Halloween and Scream one too many times," I muttered to Rusty my Heinz 57 dog and constant companion for the past six years.

But one glance at the dog, and my uneasiness turned to fear. Rusty usually enjoyed the nighttime excursions as an opportunity to run free and scour the underbrush for elusive possums and raccoons.

Not tonight.

The normally carefree dog now walked close by my side, his nose rising every few moments to sniff the smells in the wind.

"Let's hurry, Rusty," I whispered loudly to him as my sneakers churned up dust and gravel. I began to run down the winding road.

As I neared the hairpin curve, Rusty's low growl stopped me. Sliding in the gravel and falling to my knees, I glanced down at the dog as he stood glaring at the fog behind us, fur bristling down his neck and back. Hearing the grating creak of a metal gate lost somewhere in the fog, I quickly turned toward the sound, gasping as I saw the hint of a figure coming through the mist.

"Run, Rusty, run!" I screamed as I grabbed for his collar dragging him at my side.

Rusty braced himself with his four feet as I tugged.

"Let's go, Rusty. We've got to get home," I hissed as I dragged my stubborn pet.

I looked again toward the sound of the metal gate. Whatever it was that was running through the fog was coming fast. I couldn't see its form anymore. The fog seemed to have tucked it into an envelope allowing only the noises of rapid movement to escape.

Rusty held back resisting my tugging.

"You dumb dog!" I yelled. "We've got to get out of here," I said as I let go of his collar that had twisted around onto my fingers cutting off my circulation.

Rusty grabbed for my fingers with his teeth. I drew my hand back fearing that Rusty was going to bite me. Rusty reared up on his hind legs standing taller than I did. He placed a front paw on each of my shoulders and licked my face.

"Okay, Boy, I'm sorry. I know you wouldn't bite me but we've got to go that way," I said as I pointed toward the sound of the creaking metal gate.

Rusty removed his paws from my shoulders and bounced to the ground. He grabbed my fingers and gently pulled me away from the sound.

I didn't know what to do.

I trusted my best friend's instincts but I knew I had to get home and away from whatever was lumbering through the fog.

"Rusty, wait a minute. I'll come with you if you let me see who's coming through the fog after me."

Rusty looked at me and dropped his head down like he had been beaten and was cowering away from me as if I were the person doing the punishment. His tail dropped between his back legs and he whimpered.

I looked toward the bridge focusing on an area that was strangely clear of the smothering fog.

The form rose up out of nowhere to tower over the brush by the side of the road.

"It's a werewolf, Rusty. Run, Rusty, run!" I screamed as I stood in place not really believing what I was seeing or saying.

I stared at the form as it rose up even further and sniffed the air. It jerked its head around in my direction and sniffed the air again. Suddenly it let out a roar and pawed the air. A speck of light from somewhere bounced off the eyes of the form and they glistened blood red as the creeping fog covered the massive hulk, swallowing it up and leaving only the sounds of running and growling emanating from the fog.

Rusty grabbed my fingers and pulled my hand forcing me to shake myself from the frozen, shocked state I had entered.

"Let's go, Boy," I whispered to Rusty. "Let's go back home and get help."

I ran as fast as I could without looking back. Rusty was directly in front of me leading the way. Occasionally I would catch a glimpse of him turning his head toward the on-coming form. I watched him sniff the air and growl as he led our rapid retreat towards what I hoped was safety.

The fog was getting thicker and drifting to the road making our escape route more and more difficult to follow.

I knew I couldn't slow down. I could hear the heavy breathing and the slap of feet against the road behind me.

How far behind me?

I didn't know if I was losing ground to my werewolf and I was afraid to look back.

Rusty continued to lead the way but he was showing signs of slowing down. He couldn't see what was ahead of him either because of the thick blanket of fog. Only his nose was working for him and helping him lead me away from the form.

Up ahead I could finally see a clear path. At least for the moment, the fog has not enshrouded that part of the road.

"Keep going, Rusty. We should find help up ahead," I whispered between gasps for breath.

I clutched my side as a sharp pain tore through it causing tears to escape from my eyes.

"We'll make it, Boy," I encouraged Rusty as well as myself. "Not much further."

A roar rose up right behind me.

I could feel hot breath on my neck caused by my werewolf's rapid breathing and when it rose up again I could feel the air move when it swung its enormous paws in my direction trying to catch me to drag me away into the fog.

I knew I was going to die. The creature was too close.

Rusty stopped and turned to meet our attacker as he placed himself between me and my werewolf.

Suddenly a shot rang out.

I couldn't stop running; if I did, the werewolf would reach me. I couldn't tell from what direction the shot had come. If the person fired again, a bullet might hit me or, God forbid, my dog.

"Don't shoot!" I shouted but the sound rushed out in a whisper. My voice was gone. I didn't have enough air left in my lungs to force a cry for help.

A second shot rang out and I heard something fall to the ground.

I turned and saw Rusty stop dead in his tracks. He turned and moved back toward my werewolf.

"No Rusty!" I whispered harshly.

But he kept going.

"Ellen, are you all right?" shouted my concerned father.

I couldn't answer. I didn't know. The fog was moving and clearing the path behind me. I could see the form lying in a crumpled heap a few feet behind me.

"Rusty, get away from that bear!" I shouted as I fell to my knees with relief.

Darkness, being unable to see, causes the seed of fear to germinate and grow.

Dear God, how I wished my father was here to help me now.

CHAPTER 4
THE CASTLES ON WEST 14TH STREET

Mysterious notions caused fear and misunderstanding as depicted in my dream of my old neighborhood…

Tearing down the castle on West 14th Street and finding secrets was something I always thought would happen someday far in the distant future; at least, I thought so in my mind. I didn't say my thoughts out loud so anyone could hear them. I didn't really believe it would be true, not during my lifetime. I guess it seemed to me to be my writer's imagination that was doing all of the conjuring up of possibilities.

I remembered, as a kid, walking past that old wooden mansion with its round castle-like tower at each side. I was never afraid of the place like I would be of a professed haunted house. The castle seemed to give off a feeling of love and understanding. It was nothing like walking passed a cemetery. I felt peaceful and calm when I strolled in front of the great wooden structure.

Whoever owned the place put forth a great deal of effort to keep it well maintained by painting the outside of the structure every couple of years. The window glasses were spit-polish shined until the sunlight glinted off of them, fiercely blinding all who looked at it at a certain angle and a specific point in time of a sunny afternoon.

I never did know who owned the house nor did I ever see anyone who might be considered an owner. The only people I ever saw around the outside of the place were workmen dressed in the navy blue uniform type work clothes like my dad used to wear.

"Karin, do you know who owns the castle on West 14th Street?" I asked my high school chum when my curiosity got the best of me.

"There isn't a castle on West 14th Street," she said as she looked at me trying to locate my brain.

"Yeah there is. The big white house with the round towers on each side. That's the castle."

"I don't know who owns or lives there now, but my dad said West 14th Street was the affluent section of the city during the forties and earlier. That's when those big old wooden houses were built to look like castles. I wouldn't want to live in one of those places; it would be really creepy, I think."

"Why? I think it would be a fine thing to do. It would be glamorous to walk around in the footsteps of the rich and famous. It would be almost like a dream," I said as I twirled around showing all of the poise and glamour I could muster.

"Oh, I don't know. The way some of those people made their money back then wasn't very nice, you know. Seems to me like I heard about some killings that took place on West 14th Street. I don't know who it was or what it was about, but I surely wouldn't want to live there."

"You get that kind of story anywhere you live. It's especially memorable if it's about the rich and famous," I said in a rationalizing explanation.

"Yeah, I know," she agreed.

"How many of those big wooden mansions were built? Do you know?"

"I remember when I was a kid there were about four or five of them. I know two of the old houses burned down all the way to the ground. Another one was torn down for the new road. That left the two that are still standing. One was always kept in really good condition while the other one always looked like it needed a lot of repairs and definitely a new paint job."

"Who owns the old house that needs all the work?"

"The same guy who keeps the one you call the castle in such good condition also owns the run down hovel of a house."

"You're kidding? Why does he keep one of the houses in good repair and performs only necessary work on the second house?"

"I don't know," she said as she shrugged her shoulders in emphasis.

I dreaded the day the demolition would start on the house I called the castle. It was always so perfect looking but also so very empty of happy smiling faces.

The newspaper sent out reporters to cover the destruction of a monument to a time long since passed.

I took my lunch hour and stood watching the death of my dream as it toppled to the ground.

It took a couple of days to haul away the debris from the demolition.

It took many months to clear the way for any new type of construction in the same area because of a legal technicality.

It seemed that a body had been discovered in the deepest area of the debris pile.

I was there when the stir of discovery was made. I watched as workers stopped performing their tasks and removed their hats in respect to the dead body that had been unearthed. I listened as the beehive of activity was replaced with the whispers of death. I could feel the presence of death at that moment.

"Whose body is it?" I asked the person that was standing next to me along the sidewalk.

"Don't know."

"Is it a man or a woman?"

"How would I know?" the stranger answered with agitation evident in his voice.

"How long has it been there?"

"I don't know, Lady."

Of course, he didn't know. I was standing there right beside him and I didn't know either.

I knew this would happen. I knew there would be hidden secrets in that house. I just didn't know what those secrets were and how far back they traveled in time.

I scoured the newspaper daily looking for answers that didn't seem to be forthcoming. I decided to check the obituaries each day to see if there was an insert about the funeral service that would be held for the body. I wanted to know if it had been identified and what the cause of death might be.

In my heart, I wanted that body to have a name and someone who cared about whether he or she lived or died.

"Karin, have you heard anything about that body that was found under the castle on West 14th Street?"

"No, just that it was found. Why are you so interested?"

"No reason, just curiosity. I didn't know if it had been a man or woman. I thought you might have heard something?"

"No, not a word. You seem to be obsessing on that body and that house. Do you think it's somebody you know or a long gone relative?"

"I'm not from around here, remember? It's not likely to be anyone I know or that I am related to. It bothers me that no answers have been found. That's all. I'm not obsessed – just curious," I said as a weak defense to my questions of my friend.

The old man that had owned both houses, the well-kept one and the run down one, had recently died. His heirs were the ones who allowed the demolition of both of the structures that stood side by side.

Finally, when my curiosity could stand no more waiting, I wrote a letter to the editor of the newspaper. I hoped the letter would be published expressing my interest in obtaining information about the death and the surrounding circumstances.

Dear Editor:

When I first arrived in this city, I was a lost, lonely, country girl who was overwhelmed by the size of this city and the multitude of people held within its boundaries.

I would walk the sidewalks gazing at the different types of houses that had been built over the years from the oldest clapboard structures that were still standing to the newest concrete and brick facades that caused me to puzzle out the reasoning and meaning behind the building plan.

My favorite homes were the wooden castles on West 14th Street. Now, progress has deemed that these wonderful old structures be torn down and replaced with freeways.

During the destruction of one of those old homes, a body was discovered.

Has the identity been ascertained for that body and a possible reason for the death of that person who has remained hidden for so many years?

I have no ties to the homes in any way but I do think the bones should have a name.

Signed: Interested in the Truth

The editor of the newspaper published my letter without my name being added. Anyone wishing to furnish the requested information was directed to send it to the attention of the editor.

I was pleased when I saw the published letter but I really expected no response. It was my thought that eventually the legal authorities should release information to the public about the identity of the bones. I had no idea how long that would take but I didn't expect it to happen any time soon.

Well, I was wrong. Less than a week after my letter to the editor was published, someone tried to answer my questions in part via the editor.

Dear Interested in the Truth:
I was part of the work crew that discovered the body, or perhaps I should say bones. The bones had been buried in the basement of that house for many years so that left nothing for identification except possibly the DNA that could be garnered from within the bone itself. Sex was impossible to determine by those present at the discovery sight. But, based on the rotting fragment of cloth found near the bones, I would have to guess it was a woman. Age was not to be determined by us.

Just for clarification purposes, the bones were found in what used to be the basement of the house that had been kept in good condition, not the other way around, as one might have suspected.

I hope this helps a little.

Signed: Digger of the Bones

I was all smiles when I read that letter. At least, someone else besides me, a stranger, was interested in finding the truth.

I was puzzled though. I would have thought the bones would have been discovered in the basement of the house that had not been kept up to the sparkling standards of its twin structure.

Ten days later another letter to the editor was published referencing the bones.

Dear Interested and Digger:

The man who owned the houses since they were built, recently died. When he was a young man, in his teens I think, he had a twin sister who lived with him and his family. As I recall, his parents died through a wave of sickness that traveled through the city at that time leaving him and his sister to take care of each other. The dead parents had been well-to-do so that left the teenagers with no worries about money.

The tale that was told to me was that he took the money and built two identical new houses, one for his sister, and one for himself. Then, lo and behold, his sister disappeared. He explained it away as a trip to Europe followed by a marriage and then an accidental death; thus, he no longer had a sister.

I believe that if there is evidence of his DNA somewhere, that bones can be matched back to him. I believe the bones are those of his sister.

How she died is anyone's guess, but since her death was hidden, I would be inclined to think it was not one of natural causes.

I don't think the truth of her death will ever be discovered. Her name was Mary Elizabeth Szklarzinski.

Signed: Carrier of Tales

Now, we were another step closer to the truth, maybe.

It was my hope that the police department was also reading the newspaper editorial page. It appeared that I had started the snowball rolling down the hill and it was rapidly picking up speed.

Maybe with all of the advances that have been made with forensic science nowadays, an actual cause of death could be found; then again, maybe not. The bones would be able to show signs of a traumatic death if marks had been left by some kind of lethal weapon. A gun would leave a bullet hole, a knife might leave a groove or a gouge in the bone. An illness, in most cases, would leave no evidence at all.

I had resigned myself to having to accept what pieces of information I had already received as being the whole story or, at least, all that we were going to be able to get since the passing of Mary Elizabeth Szklarzinski's brother, Edward Thaddeus Szkarzinski.

It had been several months since the Carrier of Tales letter and there had been no article written about the police releasing any information about the bones. So it came as a total surprise when another letter to the editor appeared that explained more of the story of Mary Elizabeth.

Dear Editor,

I am sending this letter to you anonymously because I don't want anybody to know who I am or ask me how I should know all of this.

Mary Elizabeth Szklarzinski died of natural causes being that of pneumonia. Her tight fisted brother would not take her to see the doctor. So, Mary Elizabeth eventually drowned in her own fluids.

Edward Thaddeus was so overcome by her death that he drove himself deep into a depression that lasted until the day he died.

Edward told me that he buried his sister in the basement because he didn't want anyone to discover that he was too cheap to take her to see a doctor. He was ashamed.

There was no murder involved. Edward Thaddeus loved his sister, but he also loved his money.

He vowed to take care of her house, her final resting place, as a lasting and permanent monument to his sister.

That is why her empty house is always sparkling clean and freshly painted while his was run down and unkempt.

He had no idea that his thoughtless, unknowing descendants would allow the discovery of the bones of his much loved dead sister,

I hope this explanation will allow the twins to rest in peace.

Signed: The Truth Revealed.

I read that letter with a heart filled with sadness for both Edward Thaddeus and Mary Elizabeth Szklarzinski. She had died at a very early age but he had paid for her untimely death all of his life.

I added this last letter to the copies of the previous letters. This was a story I wanted to remember.

"Karin, have you been following the story about the castles on West 14th Street?"

"No, what about them?"

"Let's meet at The Lake Erie Restaurant tonight after work and I'll tell you all about it. I think you'll be interested in the story. We used to walk past those two houses every day on our way to school. One of them was the most elaborate headstone that was ever built on West 14th Street."

One of the deaths was an early untimely death. The second death was of old age and natural causes.

Checking on the House

That was my choice of a way to die – old age and natural, and definitely not in the trunk of my own car.

CHAPTER 5
A STUPID DREAM

Why did people always dream stupid dreams when they were in situations that seemed to be unbearable? All I could dream lately were stupid dreams. Every time I got pinched back into a hole and couldn't get out, I dreamed stupid dreams. I was tired of stupid dreams. *What can I do about it?*

I dreamed I was on the beach…

That was a stupid dream. I had never been to the beach. I had no idea what the ocean looked like other than from movies and photographs.

I dreamed I was resting on a great big old chair and my husband was right beside me. We were watching the waves as they rolled in slowly. Slowly they would come. Slowly they would go back. Then they would roll in again.

I knew I was dreaming in my dream.

It was a nice dream.

I was resting. My husband was resting. We were somewhere we had never been together.

The tide was coming in a little higher and deeper. It was lapping up the sand.

"Sonny, we've got to move," I whispered.

"Naw, we'll be just fine. It'll go back out."

"Yeah, I know, but it'll come back in, too, further the next time."

"No it won't. We'll be just fine."

That was what he usually said but I knew he was wrong. Even in my dream, I knew he was wrong.

"Sonny, we've got to move."

"No, we're okay. See, the water is going away."

"But it'll come back."

"No, I don't think so," he fell asleep immediately.

Should I listen to him? Should I get out of the way? Should I wake him up and drag him with me?

Before I could think of an answer to that question, the tide was coming back in rapidly, deeply like a giant roll.

"Sonny, wake up! Look!"

I couldn't get him awake. He wouldn't open his eyes. I shook his arm.

"Sonny, we've got to move! Look!"

He didn't wake up.

I jumped up from the chair and grabbed him. I started yanking on him.

"Let's go! Let's get out of here! Let's go! We've got to go! Sonny, please, we've got to go! Sonny! Sonny! Come on. You'll die. Sonny, you'll die."

Then the water came.

The water engulfed Sonny and didn't touch me.

It did not touch me!

It came in and scooped him up completely missing me entirely; like it was programmed not to touch the fat lady.

"Sonny, come back!"

He didn't come back.

"Sonny!"

Then I wake up. I look around. My neck is aching and my side is killing me.

I am still alive.

I'm not at the ocean.

Sonny isn't dead.

God, I hope Sonny's not dead.

I hoped that wasn't a sign. I hoped the sign wasn't telling me how much I needed to get to Roanoke and I couldn't get there.

I couldn't get to my phone.

I couldn't get out of the stupid trunk.

I heard the car door open and close gently. It was just loud enough for me to know what the sound was.

Waking up from that scary, frightful dream planted the need to go to the bathroom firmly into my head.

"John," I whispered.

No answer.

"John?"

Still no answer.

"Are you there, John?"

I was getting a little louder with each question.

"What do you want, Lady?" he growled at me.

"I need to go to the bathroom, John."

"Where do you think you're going to go to the bathroom?"

"Just let me out and go behind the car to pee. I don't want to get all soiled with urine while I'm in this trunk. Please."

"Aw cripe. Okay, Lady, I'm on my way."

I heard the car door open, gently close, and the keys jangled. John inserted the key into the trunk lock and it popped open.

I felt like I was released from a coffin.

"Here, let me help you get out," he said. He had the gun in one hand and used the other hand to provide me a brace to try to pick myself up out of the trunk.

"Thank you, John. I needed to go so badly. I just couldn't hold it any longer."

"You go right over there. I want to hear that liquid hit the ground. Do you understand me?"

"Yes, Sir. Can I stay out of the trunk now?"

"No, I just got back inside to go to sleep. You've got to go back into the trunk."

"It's like a coffin in there, John. Please let me stay out of the trunk."

"You heard what I said, Lady."

I ran over to the darkness, pulled my pants down and squatted. As soon as I pulled my pants up, I reached into my pocket, pulled my cell phone out, and inserted it in my bra.

"Thank you, John. I needed that so badly."

He had no idea how badly I needed to do that.

"Get back in the trunk, Lady."

"Okay," I said as I slowly walked over, stepped up, turned around, and scooted my backside in first so I could lift my legs up. "John, this is horrible lying back here."

"I know, Lady. I laid in your trunk quite a while myself. Just for your information, Lady, there is no way of getting out of that trunk. I've already checked it out. When I was in it, I had to leave something next to the lock or the latch so I could get back out. You don't have one of those safety release locks. How come, Lady? This is a newer car."

"I don't know. That's just the way it came. I didn't even know there was such a thing when I bought this car. Thank you for telling me. The next time I buy a car, I'll get one. I don't want to ever be in a trunk and not be able to get out."

"Too little, too late, Lady. Don't you wish you had one now?"

"Yes I do, John."

"Get in there and be quiet for a little while. I've got to go to sleep. I'm going to lay down in the back seat right next to you so I can hear every sound you make."

"Okay, John.'

I really didn't want to hear that. I would have been better off if he stayed in the front seat.

"John, you can sit in that front seat, put the seat back, and be a little more comfortable than trying to lay down in the back seat."

"No, Lady, someone is liable to see me. I would be easier to see in the front seat than in the back seat. The back seat is pointed towards the darkness more. You have a blanket back there. I can cover myself up and they won't know there is a body in the back seat of the car."

"Okay, John. Are you ever going to let me go?"

"Yeah, Lady. But I don't know how, or where, or when I'll let you go."

CHAPTER 6
THE DOOR WAS OPEN

I crawled back into the trunk and back to the memories that I wanted to tell to anyone who would listen…

The door was open. Should I go inside?

No, no, let me think about this. Mary gave me the key to the front door. Why would I need a key if she left the door open?

I stood in front of the open door while my heart was beating like a bass drum. I stared at that door hoping I would find an answer somewhere on the wood grain surface.

I stepped to one side to see if I could get a glimpse inside the house. The door wasn't open far enough. I could only see a sliver of the room on the other side of the door.

It was dark and soundless beyond the sliver – but - the door was open.

I pushed against the door softly with my fingertips. The heavy door moved only a fraction. No help, I still couldn't see inside the room enough to know what or who was lurking outside my line of vision.

Again, I pushed the door with my fingertips. It would swing no further. Something or someone was preventing it from swinging completely open.

Was it a body? Was it Mary?

"No, it couldn't be Mary lying behind that door," I whispered loudly. "Mary went to visit her sister. She couldn't be behind that door."

Standing outside the open door wondering wasn't going to find the answer for me. I had to go inside. I had to face whatever or whoever was lying in wait beyond the open door.

"Mary, Mary? Are you in there?" I shouted loudly so everybody within several hundred feet of the front door could hear me.

No response.

Of course, there was no response, Mary is out of town. What's wrong with me? Why am I such a coward?

I sucked in all the air I could get into my lungs forcing my stature higher and my shoulders straighter. Then - I pushed the door again, except this time, I placed both palms against the heavy wood and shoved hard.

"Bang!" was the noisy answer to my hearty shove. The door had swung open and crashed against the wall.

I stepped back in shock because I had not expected the door to move.

"Mary!" I yelled as I entered the house looking behind the door to see why it wouldn't open earlier. I saw nothing.

No response, only the echoes of my voice in a completely empty house as it bounced off the walls reverberating back to me.

"R-r-r-ing!" shrieked the telephone from the corner of the former living room that was now filled with only the well-worn wall-to-wall carpet and the noisy telephone.

"I should answer that."

Before I could propel myself forward to pick up the telephone receiver, the answering machine started.

"Hello, this is Mary and I'm unable to talk to you right now. Please leave your name, your number, and a brief message at the beep."

A click and a dial tone was the only thing that was recorded.

I turned and left the room, the house, and all of the imaginings that were crossing my overactive mind. I closed the door, snapping the lock into position as I pulled it softly behind me until I heard the gentle click telling me that the locking mechanism had snapped into place.

I jumped into my car and drove home with my mind jumping from one dreadful thought to another.

Why hadn't I gone into the other rooms of the house? Why didn't I check the place out to see if anything else was gone besides all the furniture in the living room?

I knew the answer to that question but I didn't want to put it into words. I didn't want my mind to formulate and voice those horrendous thoughts of finding Mary's body for fear that they might be true.

I pulled my car into my driveway and raced into the house. I was on a mission. I had to make a telephone call and I wanted to be in the comfort of my safe home when I placed that call.

I punched in the numbers and waited for the ringing to be answered on the other end of the telephone line.

"Please answer the phone. Please, please answer the phone," I whispered softly in a prayer. "Five – six – seven – eight – nine- ten, it has rung ten times. Where are you? Are you there? Is anyone there? Please answer the phone."

I placed the receiver back into its cradle.

My mind was not going to give me any peace. It was windmilling through possible scenarios of death and destruction for Mary.

"Stop it," I told myself, "you're making your own self crazy."

I picked up the telephone receiver again and held it to my ear so I could hear the loud noise of the dial tone.

"I'll prove you're wrong," I told myself and especially my overactive imagination. "You've been writing too many mysteries."

I punched in the same numbers I had tried to call earlier.

"Please answer, please, please, please,…"

"Hello."

"Oh, thank God, Mary? Is that you, Mary?"

"No, this is Emma. Mary's not here at the moment."

"Where is she?" I screamed into the telephone.

"Who is this?" demanded Emma.

"I'm so sorry. I know I sound crazy, but this is Ellen Holcombe. I'm a friend of Mary's. We work together. I really need to ask her a question. When will she be back?"

"I'm not sure."

"Please give her a message for me. Tell her to call me at this number no matter what time she gets in. She is staying with you, isn't she? Mary is your sister?"

"Yes, Mary's my sister. What's this all about?"

"I can't tell you right now. Mary will be back tonight, won't she?"

"I guess so."

"Please, please, have her call me."

I gave her my telephone number again and hung up the receiver slowly trying to figure out what had just happened.

What did she mean when she said she guessed Mary would be back tonight? Had Mary actually arrived for the visit with her sister? Or – was her sister awaiting her to appear on her doorstep? Why didn't I question Emma more?

I wandered around my small living space searching for answers from a mind that was so completely overwhelmed with fear and frustration.

I stared at my telephone, willing it to ring.

"Please call me, Mary. Please let all of the bad things that are running through my mind not be true."

The telephone rang as if on cue.

"Hello, hello, Mary? Is that you?"

"No, this is Emma. Mary hasn't arrived yet. She should be here any time but I wanted to let you know that I'm still waiting for her and I haven't forgotten your message to have her call you."

"Have you talked to her? Tonight? Have you talked to her tonight?"

"No, I haven't talked to her since yesterday."

"What time was she supposed to get there? To your house?"

"Sometime today is what she told me. Why? What's the problem?"

"I'm worried about her. She gave me her key and told me to check on her house while she was gone. I went by there earlier today and her front door was standing open. All of her living room furniture was gone. The only thing left in her living room was the telephone."

"Now, you've got me worried," said Emma in a concerned tone.

"What do you think we should do?" I sputtered into the telephone.

"Wait, I hear a car out front. Let me put this telephone down for a moment and check on it, okay?"

"Sure, go ahead."

I wanted to crawl through that telephone line and see for myself who had pulled into Emma's driveway.

I could hear a muffled conversation.

"What took you so long?"

"Traffic and I told you I was going to make a few stops on the way here."

"Ellen Holcombe is on the telephone. Over there, see it? Pick it up and talk to her. She was worried to death about you."

"Why?"

"Just answer the phone."

"Is there anything wrong, Ellen?"

"I was worried about you, Mary," I said with a burst of all run together words.

"Why? I told you I was going to visit Emma."

"Yes, I know, but when I checked on your house, the front door was standing open and all of your living room furniture was gone, and I was too afraid to look through the rest of the house. I was sure I was going to find a body, your dead body."

"When are you going to put a rein on that writer's imagination of yours? I was having my carpet cleaned. The men doing the job probably left the front door unlocked. That's why I wanted you to check on my place. All the living room furniture is in the spare bedroom."

"Oops, I'm sorry, Mary. Tell Emma to forgive me. Bye," I smiled as I cradled the telephone receiver.

"This will make a great story," I whispered with a smile.

Maybe it was a good thing that I was a writer and my imagination was ripe, perhaps overripe.

CHAPTER 7
WHERE AM I?

I was trying to wake up. I could feel my eyelids as they pulled and tried to open up to let in the light.

I knew my eyes were open. I was blinking so I knew my eyes were open, but I couldn't see anything.

I tried to bring my hands to my face but I couldn't seem to get both arms up anywhere near my head.

What is happening to me? Why can't I see anything? Why can't I move my arms to my head? Where am I?

"Where am I?" I shouted in my head – no maybe I said that out loud. "Where am I?" I screamed again.

I blinked my eyes until I felt as though I was going to pass out.

Then it filtered into my tired brain that I was still in the trunk of my own car.

Did I say those words out loud? If I did, why didn't he tell me to shut up? I must have dreamed I said those words.

I had to move around. My body was getting numb on my right side. I needed to get off my right side. The only way I could do that was flop around and try to roll over facing away from the trunk opening.

If I did that, I would make too much noise. *What will he do if I make too much noise?*

Who is going to hear me? I was in the trunk of a car parked in an area where there were no other cars around. Who is going to hear me make noise?

John is; that's who.

"God, Ellen, you're so stupid sometimes," I told myself in an ugly tone.

Suddenly the trunk lid rose.

"What is it that you're doing in there?" came a harsh whisper.

"My side is killing me. I'm trying to turn over to the other side. It sure would help if you would let me get out of here," I pleaded without any shame.

"Okay, Lady, get out of there and get into the car. You drive. You aren't going to let me sleep with all of the racket you keep making."

I climbed out slowly. He didn't give me a hand that time and it was a struggle trying to straighten out some of my cramped up appendages.

As with little old ladies when they reach my age, I had to go to the bathroom.

"I've got to go over there again," I said as I pointed to the darkness.

"Hurry up, please," he whispered at me.

After taking care of the necessary job, I walked slowly to the car and climbed into the driver seat.

Nature must have yanked on John's chain because as he walked toward the passenger side of the car, he was zipping up his jeans.

I had no plan. All of that time in the trunk and I thought of nothing that would help me get away from my abductor.

I started the engine, shifted the car into gear, and drove off without the headlights.

Once off of the parking lot, I turned on the headlights and turned the car toward the direction from where I had come. He didn't seem to notice and I wasn't about to tell him.

I was driving along the deserted city streets trying to find an on ramp to the freeway that would lead me to Roanoke.

He obviously wasn't paying any attention to where I was driving. His only need or desire was that I drove.

"Where to, John?" I asked softly so I wouldn't get him too interested in the road ahead of us.

"Just keep driving. I'll tell you when to stop," he answered me in a stern tone.

So far so good, I thought as I tried to maintain the proper speed.

A vibration, a noise, a buzzing sound radiated from my bra.

My cell phone had come to life.

Someone was trying to call me.

I didn't want John to hear the buzz so I rolled down the window to create a noise from the draft of the moving car.

"What are you doing, Lady?"

"What do you mean?" I asked hoping he was not questioning the buzz.

"The window, what are you trying to do? Freeze me to death?"

"I'm sleepy. I need the cool air to keep me awake," I answered trying to think fast so I could keep the window open until the buzzing stopped.

I wanted to reach into my bra, grab that phone, flip it open, and scream for help.

I knew I couldn't do that. It might be my husband and if I gave him any indication that I needed help, he would get too excited, and he could have more major heart problems.

If it was one of my sons, he could get help for me, but I couldn't answer my phone.

"Lady, what's that up ahead?"

"A tunnel."

"We went through two of those tunnels a couple of hours ago. How many of those monsters do you have in this area?"

"A few. I'm not real sure how many," I said in response as I lied through my teeth.

"This one looks like the last one we went through," he said as he sat up straighter in his seat and looked around.

"They all look alike to me," I answered quickly.

The truth was that it was the same tunnel and tunnels gave me the heebie-jeebies, especially this tunnel with which I was a little more familiar than I cared to be.

CHAPTER 8
THE TUNNEL

My mind spun around and around until it stopped on a memory…

The town looked deserted as it should at two in the morning. I didn't even see a police car patrolling the area in search of suspects of nefarious deeds in the night.

I didn't want to be the only human being wandering around in the dead of night with only the weak, wavering street lights to help guide me.

It was my fault. It was all my fault. I shouldn't have gotten out of the car so far away from home.

Well, on second thought, maybe I did do the right thing. After all, I think the guy was driving me out into the middle of nowhere to rape me. I was sure of that, deep down in my bones, I was sure that had been his plan the whole evening.

Now, I was out and alone and afraid of what the darkness might hold within each shadow that was not reached by the street lights. There were plenty of those, shadows I mean.

I saw a four-county bus. The bus route covered parts of four different counties, thus the name.

I didn't think they ran on the roads at night. I waved like a crazy woman at the driver.

"I'm not picking up passengers," said the man as he pulled to a stop in front of me. He didn't have much choice in the matter. I was standing in the middle of the road and I wasn't going to move.

"Please, Mister, I need a ride back to Stillwell," I pleaded.

"I'm only going to the tunnel that leads to Bluefield. I'll have to let you out there."

"That's great. That's a little closer to home. I'll take any ride I can get as long as I don't have to - - never mind," I said as I tried to shake off the thought. "How much, Mister?"

"Nothing, you look like you could use a little help," he answered with a sigh.

I found a seat to the right of the driver so I could still see him and not just the back of his head that would be my view on the other side of the bus.

It didn't take long to drive the ten miles to the tunnel.

"This is the end of the line, Lady," he said as he roused me from my dream with his booming voice.

"Oh, okay, thanks," I said as I stood up and tried to gather my wits about me. I must have dozed off in the few minutes I was sitting on the warm, cozy, safe bus.

"Watch your step and be careful," he shouted as he closed the door of the bus.

I looked around me and, once again, discovered that I was alone. Because this was the entrance to the East River Mountain Tunnel, I would have thought someone would have been around for safety sake, but I saw absolutely no one.

At least, there was light outside and inside the tunnel.

Big deal, if no safety personnel were around and someone tried to grab me, what difference would the lights make?

You'd think there would be a car or two coming through here.

Is the thing blocked? Have they closed it on the other side?

There were no vehicles approaching the entrance to this tunnel or exiting the second tunnel that housed the next two lanes.

I could just sit there and wait for whatever could happen to happen. Or, I could start walking through this monstrosity that I was told was over a mile in length so I could get to the other side and closer to home as soon as possible.

I decided to walk.

The tunnel always made me nervous. When I would have to drive through it, images of gigantic cave-ins or fierce explosions would race through my brain in brutal Technicolor.

There is a narrow walkway built on one side of the two lane tunnel that allowed foot traffic to safely pass through the confines of the tunnel without the fear of being struck by a passing vehicle. I was sure that foot traffic was not an everyday happening. It should only occur in the event of an emergency.

Well, I guess my problem could qualify as an emergency. All I wanted to do was go home.

I was in a quandary as to what I should do in the event a vehicle happened to pass through the tunnel.

Should I jump up and down and scream? Or, should I shrink myself up into the smallest piece of human flesh I could imagine and make no attempt to be noticed?

Walk, that's what I had to do – just walk.

The light was strange inside the tunnel. It looked bright when I entered it at night, but in actuality, it was hard to see where I was going. I kept my hand sliding along the guardrail.

The sounds were strange and frightening. I couldn't tell what was causing the different noises because the sounds would echo and reverberate throughout the entire tunnel. I couldn't tell if the sounds were in front of me or behind me. I had no idea what they were.

I kept walking, guiding my progress with the guardrail.

A few feet beyond a mile, that's all the longer this tunnel is. I can walk a mile in my sleep. I do it almost every day at the Little League Park not too far from my office.

I could feel the rumbling of a vehicle.

"Where is it?" I cried aloud as I propelled my body to turn completely around where I stood. "There it is," I shouted as I pointed at two headlights coming toward me.

I couldn't tell how fast the headlights were speeding toward me. I couldn't tell what kind of vehicle was behind those bright lights. All I knew at that particular moment was that I was no longer alone.

"Oh, God, what if it's that fool that I am running away from? What can I do? Where can I hide?"

That was a stupid question. There was absolutely no place to hide except in the shadows. As soon as those headlights came a little closer, there would be no shadows.

I saw a lip or an extension of the wall just ahead. Maybe I could flatten myself against the corner and disappear. Then again, maybe not.

If I scooted down on the other side of the lip and planted myself as close to the bottom of the shelf on which the walk way was built, maybe I would be harder to see.

No, won't work, that only puts my body down closer to eye level in a car.

Maybe it's not a car. Maybe it's a truck, a semi. In that case, I would want the driver to see me and hopefully offer to help me.

The headlights were getting closer and I was wedged up, standing as straight as I could, against the extension in the wall. I closed my eyes, held my breath, and waited for what, I didn't have a clue.

The vehicle stopped next to me.

I could see the flashing of bright lights and no lights and bright lights and no lights from underneath my closed eyelids.

"Ma'am, do you need help?" asked a concerned voice.

I finally opened one eye to see the flashing blue lights of a State Police car.

"Yes, Officer, I need to get home," I said as the tears flowed down my cheeks.

"Are you hurt? Do you need to go to the hospital?" he asked as he spotted the tears.

"Only my pride, Sir. All I need is a ride to a telephone so I can call someone to give me a ride home."

"Why are you out here walking through this tunnel?"

"Well, I had a dinner meeting, not actually a date that was turning into something a little more physical than I wanted it to be so I took off walking. I sure am glad you came along. I was so scared. I had no idea how frightening this tunnel could be at night. I don't like driving through it in the daylight. Walking through it at night is not something I care to repeat ever again."

"Jump down from there, get in the car, and I'll take you to headquarters where you can call for a ride. The next time, maybe you should get yourself a cell phone, just in case."

"Yes, Sir, I will do that. I'll do something even better than that. The next time, I'll drive my own car and I won't have to do anything I don't want to do to earn my ride back home."

As the officer drove me through the remainder of the East River Mountain Tunnel, I saw the car I had jumped out of drive past slowly looking for me. I was sure of it.

I was so happy to be in the back of that police car and safely out of the reach of my rape date.

I never told Sonny about my excitement in the tunnel. I never told him it was a person I worked with that had ideas of rape in his mind.

Needless to say, that coworker quit his job and moved on to new pastures. I'm sure he was worried that I would talk.

He didn't know that I couldn't tell anybody about the encounter because of Sonny and his heart condition. He could have stayed in the area and proceeded to attack other women without any interference from me.

I couldn't afford to get embroiled in an ugly court case, not without hurting Sonny.

I knew my coworker would try to make the whole episode appear to be my fault. That always happens with those kinds of court cases.

I knew it wasn't me who stirred him up other than the fact that I was a woman; a fat woman, at that.

That wasn't the only time I had to run from a man.

CHAPTER 9
WHILE YOU WERE OUT

Sonny was not my first husband. That claim to fame belonged to Edward, the father of my two sons...

WHILE YOU WERE OUT was printed across the top of the small piece of pink paper in bold letters as a warning to be noticed and acted upon immediately. There was no one in the outside world that should be calling me for any reason. It wasn't about my boys, I had already checked on them. They were fine, no problems there.

I moved the message aside, putting it out of my sight at least for the moment, but I knew I shouldn't ignore it.

I tried to keep my mind focused on my work that was spread out before me.

WHILE YOU WERE OUT swirled around in my head blocking out any hope of concentrating on the accounting figures that I needed to crunch into an understandable report.

I reached for the menacing little pink note and started to crumple it and toss it into the waste basket. I could say I didn't see the message. It would be a lie but, at least, it would buy me some time.

Why should I say anything? It shouldn't be him because he didn't know where I was. If I ignored the message, maybe he would go away and not turn my life upside down again. I didn't want to talk with him- no way, shape, or form.

How did he find me? I didn't tell anyone where I was, not even my mother and father.

I held the small pink piece of paper in front of me so I could read the telephone number.

It's a local number. He's here.

I glanced around me half way expecting him to be standing behind me ready to spring at me at any second.

I kept my head low behind the barricade of file cabinets that surrounded me and blocked me from view from the hallway.

"What am I going to do?" I asked myself in a barely audible whisper.

I knew I had to get out of there. I had to gather what belongings I could grab at a moment's notice, pick up my sons from the baby-sitter, pile everything into the old, beat-up, white Plymouth, and drive as far and as fast as I was able to drive in a day.

"If he found me, did he find my sons?" I asked in a panic as I started writing a note that I would leave sitting on my desk for anyone to see if they were looking for me. The note was directed to Mr. Burton, my boss for about twelve months. That's the longest amount of time my boys and I have been able to stay anywhere without the threat of Ed looming large in our lives.

Dear Mr. "B",

Someone from my past has reared his ugly head and, again, I must run for cover dragging with me my two sons.

Please forgive me for leaving you without a reasonable notice.

My last paycheck should be mailed to the home of my mother and father. You will find the address on my application. I will retrieve it from them as soon as I can.

It has been a pleasure to know you and the Mrs. and I know a nicer group of people can't be found than those I have worked with for the last twelve months.

Forgive me,

Ellen

I scrawled my name across the bottom of note, sealed it in an envelope on which I had written "Attention: Mr. B." As I was placing the envelope in an obvious spot on my desk, I heard a familiar voice.

"I'm looking for Ellen Hutchins. Where might she be?"

The voice was distinctive with the tones permanently etched into my brain. I knew it was him. I had to get away before he wormed his way back into my life. He figured out that I had taken back my maiden name.

I ducked my head below the partition and sneaked out carrying my coat and handbag. I spoke to no one. I acknowledged no one. I kept my eyes trained on the path that would lead me away from him.

I ran through the expansive parking lot to my car where I jabbed the key into the lock and started the engine before I was actually seated. I rammed the gear shift into reverse and tore out of the parking lot like I was being chased by a demon.

I glanced in the rearview mirror every few seconds trying to determine whether or not I was being followed. I didn't want to lead him to my boys. I drove a round-about route to get to them just to be sure.

"Jenny, Jenny," I said as I ran to the front door of my baby-sitter's house. "Jenny, please be here and have my boys with you. Please, Jenny, please," I said as I banged on the front door as hard as I could.

The door opened slowly and I could tell they were gone. He had taken my sons. He had stolen my life and my reason for living.

"What did you do?" I pleaded with Jenny as she stepped back to let me enter.

"I let the boys leave with their daddy. They called him daddy and hugged him when he told them to do it. They didn't want to do it, at first, but they finally hugged him. He took hold of them and left."

"Why didn't you tell him to get out?"

"There was no way I could stop him, Ellen," she cried as she collapsed onto the sofa.

"Did you call the cops?"

"He told me not to or else. I didn't know what 'or else' meant. I didn't want to find out, Ellen. He was a crazy man."

"What did he say he was going to do?"

"He didn't. He just took Eddy and Aaron and left. He told me, again, not to call the cops. He didn't say it in a nice way."

"Did he say where he was going?"

"He said he was going to find you."

"Did you tell him where I work?"

"No, he already knew."

"What kind of car was he driving?"

"It was medium blue with Pennsylvania plates. I think it was a Chevy, late model."

"The plates will stick out like a sore thumb around here. Maybe I'll be able to find him. I hope he hasn't left this area yet. I hope he is still here so I can get my boys back."

"How are you going to find him?"

"I'm going to drive around for a while. I'm not calling the police, not yet anyway, because he is so unpredictable. He might hurt my sons."

"Call me later, okay?"

"Why?"

"I want to help, that's all."

"You've already helped enough," I said as I tried to control the venom filtering through my system.

I ran to my car and jumped into the seat where I sat and stared through blinding tears at nothing in particular. In my mind I was seeing my sons being whisked away to a faraway place that I would never be able to find.

I shook my head to remove the thought of the horrible loss. I couldn't give up. I had struggled too hard and too long to keep my sons safe from the violence offered to them by their father.

When I married Ed, I had no idea that he had a hidden dark side that erupted full force when he lost his temper. His way of solving a problem, any problem, was to reach out and hit me or his sons.

The day I discovered the bruise on Eddy's bottom that was shaped like Ed's boot toe, was the day I determined to rid myself and my sons of his violence.

It took a few more months, but we managed to disappear from his violent reach.

"Mom, Dad, the boys and I need a place to live. We've got to get away from Ed before he really hurts us," I told my parents when I appeared with bags in hand on their doorstep late one night.

"Sure, Honey, come on in. We'll get a place fixed right up for you three to sleep."

Ed found me two days later and would not stop harassing my mom and dad. He called at all hours of the day and night. He banged on the door and caused disturbances for which the neighbors called the sheriff. Before the authorities arrived, Ed left and all was calm and quiet again.

The boys and I packed up again and I started driving south.

At first, I thought he wanted the three of us to return home and resurrect our family, but I was so very wrong. He only wanted the boys.

He also had another agenda. He wanted to see me struggle under the weight of the pain and guilt he planned to heap onto my back for keeping his precious sons away from him. His goal in life was to see me crumple into a heap of mental anguish.

I wasn't going to let him do it. I wasn't going to let him punish Eddy and Aaron because he was angry with me and my efforts to stop him from seeing the boys.

I had to find him. I knew he wouldn't leave the area until he had the opportunity to gloat.

I drove around for a couple of hours without any luck at finding a car with Pennsylvania plates. My next thought was to go home and wait for him to call or show up on my doorstep.

Before I arrived home, I made a stop at the sheriff's office where I displayed my custody papers and told them that my ex-husband had stolen my sons. My thought was that they should put a deputy on my street where he could watch for the arrival of Ed.

The slow moving seconds led to even slower minutes that finally, at long last, passed into painfully long hours as I paced the floor waiting for him to brag. He had to brag. There was nothing else he could do to satisfy himself. He had to have the last word. It was inevitable that he had to brag.

While waiting and to offset the pacing, I packed clothing into suitcases and toys into any boxes I could locate. I would have to leave most of the items the boys and I had collected for the last year but that couldn't be helped. We had to get away from Ed.

I carried all of the packed and boxed items out to the car while I waited for Ed to begin his bragging. It was just a matter of time. It was going to happen. He couldn't leave without getting into my face.

It was getting dark so I turned on every light in the house. If he was going to appear before me, I wanted to make sure I was able to get a good look at him. If the bragging escalated into something worse, I hoped someone outside would be able to see the something worse as it occurred.

I turned on the television to help me pass the time. The waiting was wearing my nerves really thin.

I heard a vehicle slow down and stop in front of my house. A car door slammed followed by the sound of footsteps on the sidewalk.

It had to be him.

I made myself remain sitting on the sofa. I wasn't going to jump up and run to the window to see if it was him.

"Ellen, open the door," screamed Ed as he banged on the flimsy front door with his fists.

"Okay, give me chance to get there," I screamed back at him. He had scared me with the sudden loud banging and the fear forced me to scream back at him. I didn't want to do that. I didn't want him to know what he was doing to me.

I struggled with the lock, trying to turn it as he pushed against the door trying to force his way inside my house.

"Back off, Ed," I shouted. "I can't turn the lock with you pushing on the door."

The lock finally turned and he almost fell into the room because he was in such a rush to get inside the door.

"Did you lose something, Ellen?" he asked with an ugly smirk covering his face.

"No, not that I know," was my stupid answer.

"I found two little boys, I thought maybe you lost them."

"You stole them, Ed. I didn't lose anything."

"Well, we are going to Pennsylvania, my sons and me, where we will become one big happy family."

"No, you're not, Ed. I'll see you dead before I allow Eddy and Aaron to join your big happy family."

"How are you going to do that, Ellen?"

"Well, Ed, I don't really want you dead. I don't know how I would explain it to the boys. I would like to see you spend a nice long time behind bars so you could think about what kind of person you have become."

"That's not going to happen, Ellen. No cop is going to lock me up for wanting to take care of my kids."

"No cop would do that where we used to live, Ed. All of your buddies on the police force there would just tell you to behave and let you go. Now, you aren't where you will be protected, are you? You don't have your buddies to help you, do you?"

"I don't need any help."

"How did you find us, Ed?"

"The Internet. It's amazing what you can find on that wonderful network of information. If you use it just once, you then become a piece of information that can be tracked. It was easy, Ellen."

"Where are the boys?"

"They are safe where you can't get at them."

"Where are they," I screamed in a panic.

The scream must have aroused the deputy. He exited his vehicle with his gun drawn and came running up to my front door.

Ed was shocked to see that I had gone so far as to have a deputy sheriff lurking on the sidelines.

"What's he here for?" Ed demanded as he glared at me.

"He is going to protect me and my sons and arrest you for child stealing, kidnapping, or whatever it takes to get you to leave us alone."

"You can't arrest me for taking care of my own flesh and blood sons."

"Yes, Sir, we can," explained the deputy slowly as he forced Ed to turn around and place his hands behind his back. "According to the document that this lady has, she has full and complete custody. You don't even have visitation rights unless you are supervised. Now, where are the children?"

"I can't tell you that."

"Ed, please don't leave them with strangers. Tell me where they are so I can bring them back home," I pleaded through a waterfall of frightened, angry tears.

"Mister, make it easier on yourself and tell me where the children are being held," demanded the deputy sheriff.

"You will give them back to her," he answered angrily as he snapped his head in the direction of where I was standing. "She is an unfit mother and wife. She should consider herself lucky to be alive. Never should she be allowed to take care of my sons. They would be better off dead."

"What have you done with them? You didn't hurt Eddy and Aaron, did you?" I screamed at him as I beat on his chest with my fists while the deputy watched.

"They are fine, for now."

"What do you mean, for now?" I screamed in his face.

"Just what I said, for now. That's all I mean," he answered with an ugly smirk.

"How did you get here?" I asked as I tried to harness my anger and control my terror.

"Ask your buddy. He was watching. He knows."

I looked at the deputy.

"A cab, he arrived in a cab."

"Where's your car?" I asked softly.

"Parked."

"Where is it parked?"

"I forget."

"Are the boys with your car, in a motel room, or what?" I asked harshly.

"I forget."

"We're not getting anywhere with this," said the deputy as he started shoving Ed out the door. "I'm taking him to the sheriff's office where he can be dealt with properly."

"I'll follow you," I shouted as I grabbed my handbag and locked the front door.

There can't be that many places he could stay in this area, can there? If he took a cab, he had to be picked up somewhere first, where? Where is his car? Are the boys locked up in the car? Is someone else involved in this? Are my sons safe?

I was driving myself crazy with the swirling unanswered questions.

At the sheriff's office, things did not get better. Ed spoke no words except to say, "I want a lawyer."

The descriptions of my sons were given to the other deputies and a search was begun with all the deputies looking for a blue vehicle with Pennsylvania plates.

They expected me to go to the house where I was told to sit and wait for the results of the searching.

I couldn't do that.

I couldn't sit and wait.

I had to do something.

I had to find my boys.

Most of my night had been spent wasting time at the sheriff's office but with the morning light came my opportunity to search.

I started driving, looking for places Ed could stay overnight with two little boys. I was looking for places where he could hide his car from the road. I was looking for any type of hole he could crawl into to keep out of sight.

When I arrived at a cluster of houses, I climbed from my car and wandered around on foot peering into places where I couldn't drive my vehicle.

After satisfying myself that his car wasn't hidden anywhere around the cluster of houses, I would proceed on to the next search site.

I knew I was looking into areas that the cops wouldn't be allowed to look without a search warrant but that was the only way I would be able to know for sure that my boys weren't hidden there.

The minutes were ticking by fast now, too fast. I knew I was going to lose my boys if I didn't hurry and find them. I didn't know where Ed had them hidden, but I knew they might die.

Why did I know they might die? No reason, except that he was so unpredictable when he was angry and he was angry enough with me not to care whether his sons lived or died. His only goal would be that I not get them back.

The deputies wouldn't have any idea how desperate I was for their safety. They could only see an upset, frustrated mother who lost her little boys.

I searched and searched along the road that led into town. Next I would have to spread out and follow some of the county roads into some more isolated areas but first I wanted to see a telephone book.

When I moved to this area, I was told about a motel that was not located along the well-traveled path that led to town.

I stopped at a convenience store and asked to see the phone book.

The Just Like Home Motel was located on Route 139, one of those county roads that led to nowhere in particular.

That was where he parked his car. Deep down in my soul I knew it was there. The only problem was how was I going to find it?

"Sir, how do I get to Route 139?" I asked the elderly man behind the counter.

"You got family that way?"

"Not really, I'm trying to find the Just Like Home Motel."

"You got business at that place?"

"No, I'm looking for someone. I think he might have stayed there."

"That's a bad place, Young Lady."

"I really need to find it, Sir. Could you tell me how to get there?" I pleaded.

"Stay on this road for another mile. The turn off to 139 is on your left. I wouldn't go there if I was you. Not a good idea. You seem to be a nice lady. Don't go there."

"I have to, Sir. I don't really have a choice," I said as I walked away from the elderly man who stood watching me and shaking his head negatively.

The motel was a dirty speck in the eye of humanity.

I could feel eyes following my every move as I drove onto the pot-holed parking lot that was located in the front of the ramshackled, old building. I could see a well-worn driving path to the back of the building but I thought I would check with the manager, if there was one, before I stuck my nose and car where it didn't belong.

A woman dressed in blue jeans and a tee shirt was behind the counter when I entered the office.

"I'm looking for Ed Sklarz," I said as I stood in front of the counter.

"There's no one here by that name."

"He was here though, wasn't he? When did he check out?"

"Who are you?" demanded the blue jeaned woman.

"I'm his wife and the mother of the two little boys that were staying with him."

"I don't know who you're talking about. There is no one here by that name."

"Okay, he's not here now. But, has he been here?"

"I don't have to answer that question, Lady. You aren't the cops and I don't see a warrant in your hand."

"Fine, don't answer me. The sheriff will be your next visitor."

I stormed out the door, climbed into the car, and fought back the angry tears. I started the engine and drove to the back of the building where I found a blue car with Pennsylvania plates parked so that it couldn't be seen from the road. I jumped out of my car and walked around Ed's vehicle as I peered inside to see if my boys were there.

I could hear whimpers from a child coming from the car but I couldn't see him.

"Eddy, Aaron, where are you?" I screamed.

"Mommy, Mommy, help us!"

"Where are you?"

"In the back, the trunk. Help us!" screamed Eddy through the sobs.

"Okay, Baby. I'll get you out."

I looked around for something, anything that I could use to pry open the trunk. I ran to the trunk of my car and located a tire iron.

I fought hard trying to force the end of the tool under the lid far enough to give me some leverage to pull open the trunk near the lock.

"Mommy, hurry!" screamed Aaron.

"I am, Baby. Just one more minute."

Finally the lid popped open and my dirty, scared little boys popped up from the trunk.

I put both boys in my car and started driving. I wanted to get far away before I called the sheriff and let him know where I found my boys. I knew my ex-husband would be released and I didn't want him to be able to find me and my sons.

"Sheriff, I found my sons locked in the trunk of my ex-husband's car."

"Where are you now, Ms. Hutchins?"

"I'm not going to tell you, Sheriff. When he gets out, he will find me. I want to get a running start to get away from him, if you know what I mean."

"We can prosecute him, Ms. Hutchins."

"Sure, you can. Then he will get out of jail again. He won't stop looking for me, not ever, not until the day he dies."

"Get a restraining order."

"A piece of paper won't work. I've tried that before, Sheriff. I've got to go. My boys and I have a long drive ahead of us."

"You need to stay around so you can be a witness against your ex-husband."

"I can't, Sheriff. He might succeed the next time. Good-bye and thanks for trying to help."

I hung up the telephone. My two young sons and I disappeared from Ed's life until my sons were old enough to want to see him on their own after reaching adulthood. Then it became their choice, not mine.

CHAPTER 10
WINDOW WATCHING

I had more than my share of ugly male/female relationships. Until I met Sonny, I was afraid to begin a relationship with any man for fear the outcome would be ugly.

Even with Sonny at my side, I seemed to attract all of the crazies in the world.

"What are you looking at?" asked Sonny as his curiosity got the best of him.

"Nothing in particular, just looking."

"You act like it's the most important thing in the world, riding around at night, especially on a hot night."

"I like to look inside the houses at night. It's fun to peer inside a neighbor's house. Especially the ones that you know you'll never be invited to visit. You can get an idea of what kind of people they are by the way they live."

"You're just being nosey."

"Yeah, I guess I am. But what harm does it do?"

"None, I guess. Are you about ready to go on home?"

"Sure, but drive a little slower will you? Sometimes you fly down this road and I can't see a thing."

"That's the whole idea," Sonny mumbled.

Sonny did slow his speed a little but not enough to help my window watching.

Most of the time the windows I peered into, the ones that had opened blinds or had curtains pulled to the side, were illuminated by a bright light suspended from the ceiling or lamps located on end tables.

Never would I myself allow a stranger to peer through an illuminated window into my house and into my world uninvited. My world was private and no unwanted, uninvited outsiders were welcomed at any time. I couldn't imagine why people would want to light up their private lives for the world to see. I allowed only shadows to be seen by the outside world.

The heat had been sweltering, in the eighties most of the day, and night time didn't bring with it much improvement. Humidity or not, the curtains should be drawn, the blinds should be closed, or the shades should be pulled regardless of the heat. At the very least, all lights inside the house should be extinguished so that no unwelcome, peering eyes could penetrate the dweller's life. I had, on occasion, opened my windows wide to permit the night air to enter, but allowed no light from inside the house to illuminate my private world unless the shades were pulled.

Not everyone felt the same way I did. I wouldn't be enjoying the hobby of window watching if everybody followed my rules.

My eyes held a steady stare as I watched for uncluttered windows into another world.

Through one window I saw a child sitting on a sofa rubbing what looked to be a toy across the seat cushion. It was probably a little toy car. I remembered when my boys had done the same thing.

The next window presented the bright flashings of a television screen as it changed from a light scene to a darker, more subdued scene.

The darkness seemed to have slipped up on everybody that night because I was getting views into a lot of the worlds I had never entered previously.

The next panoramic view was void of human beings or any type of flashing television screens. There was a sofa and an end table that held a tall lamp emitting a dim light.

There was a large sofa-sized picture above the sofa but all I was able to distinguish was the gold-colored frame as the glint of the dim light glanced off of it radiating the shiny beauty.

I looked down for a moment because Sonny was driving past a wooded area where there were no houses. When I looked up to continue my window watching, I caught a flash at one side of the window.

I saw the body fall.

"Sonny, I just saw somebody get shot," I whispered excitedly.

"What did you say?"

"I saw somebody get shot."

"You couldn't have."

"But I did. I saw the flash of a gun and then the body fell."

"You're kidding, aren't you?"

"No, I'm not kidding. What should we do?"

"About what?"

"I saw somebody get shot."

"Did you see who did the shooting?"

"No, I only saw the flash of the gun."

"Did you see who got shot?"

"No, just a falling body."

"They'll think you're crazy if you report this. What are you going to tell them?" he paused as if waiting for me to answer. "How about this? I was snooping in somebody else's business when I didn't belong there and I think I saw something I shouldn't have seen."

"Sonny, it was at that house, the first one past that wooded area."

"Forget about it, Ellen. It was just your eyes and your imagination playing tricks on you."

"I know what I saw, Sonny. I'm not crazy."

I did not say another word about what I knew I saw. What was the use? Sonny wasn't going to believe what I told him. I wasn't sure I believed what I told him.

The night was long and mostly sleepless. Every time I closed my eyes, the flash and the falling body appeared in my memory like a videotape that was rewound and played again and again.

I strained each time I saw the flash to see the hand that held the gun, or maybe the arm that was extended in front of the shooter. It was useless; all I saw in any of the replays was the flash.

I focused on the body. It was a body. Wasn't it? How was it dressed? Was it a man or a woman? How could I be sure it was really a person that fell to the floor? What else could it have been?

My dreams were not supplying me any answers. When I awoke I had a lot of questions, more questions than I had before I closed my eyes.

On my way to work at the school board office, my husband had to drive past the house that had haunted my dreams all night long.

"Look, Sonny, the drapes have been closed."

"It's early, Ellen. Many people aren't even out of bed yet. They wouldn't have a reason to open their drapes yet."

"They weren't closed last night. That's why I saw the shooting."

"You saw something, Ellen. I'll grant you that much. I don't think you saw what you think you saw."

"But I did, Sonny. I swear I did see someone get shot."

Sonny drove on to the office where he deposited me at the front door.

I grabbed the two daily newspapers that had been tossed onto the porch before I unlocked the door to let myself inside where I would be alone for at least an hour. I was always the first to arrive and I liked the solitude and silence before I started my busy workday.

I started to lay the newspapers aside when I saw the headlines.

SHOOTING IN STILLWELL COUNTY

"I did see it," I whispered as I sat on the bench in the lobby to read beyond the headlines.

The body of a woman was found on Trash Dump Road. No identification was found around or on the body so the Stillwell County Sheriff's Department is asking for your help in identifying her.

The woman appears to be in her mid-thirties, weighing approximately 120 lbs., and standing about 5'4" tall. She has blonde hair and green eyes.

A photograph or artist's rendering is not available at this time.

"Did I see a woman?" I asked myself when I finished the article.

The person I saw shot was in a house located on Fairgrounds Road that was about fifteen miles from Trash Dump Road.

"Is it the same person?" I muttered to myself as I started my early morning duty of making coffee.

The school board office was located in what used to be a mansion of by-gone days. In reality, it was a large house, not an office. When the school board acquired the house, they put forth every possible effort to preserve the original appearance of the interior structure. The offices were actually bedrooms. Large ballrooms and parlors were partitioned into smaller offices that created a hodge-podge of room sizes and hallways.

I heard a door open and close quietly. It struck me as odd because my coworkers usually let everything slam and bang upon entry into the building.

"Doris? Is that you?"

No answer.

Footsteps. I felt them rather than heard them. It was almost like a stirring of the air or a reformation of the air particles.

The skin on my arms was rising in a multitude of tiny bumps as a chill of fear caressed me with its icy presence.

I ducked into a stairway that was designed to look like a closet. I was afraid to flip the light switch because of the loud snap that would be created.

The stairway was narrow and very steep. It had been built for the use of the servants when the house was constructed and in later years fashioned into office space.

I placed my hands each against a side wall and carefully felt with my foot the next step. Slowly I moved down the staircase hoping that nothing had been stacked on the steps for storage.

When I reached the first floor, the darkness was pressing on me like a weight. I needed to get out of the closet stairway and into an area that was more open and inviting.

I felt myself holding my breath. I was afraid that the person, who was not Doris, might hear me.

Sweat was beginning to moisten my brow despite the chill bumps that covered my arms. I strained to hear a noise. All I could hear was my own breathing and my heart pounding in my chest like a bass drum.

I stood behind the door that led into the hallway and to the back door. The back door would lead me to safety.

Except that maybe he was outside waiting for me. I couldn't go outside. I couldn't take that chance.

Suddenly the back door opened and someone entered the hallway that was on the other side of the door from where I was standing. That someone wasn't even pretending to be quiet.

"Doris? Is that you?" I asked in a barely audible whisper.

The door behind which I had been hiding suddenly opened filling the area with bright light.

"Ellen, what are you doing in there? Are you all right? You're as white as a ghost."

"Hi, Doris. I thought I heard something in here so I was checking it out."

"In the dark."

"Yeah, well, if it was a mouse or rat, it wouldn't come out if the light was on."

"If you say so," said Doris as she stared at me. "Are you sure you're all right?"

"Yes, no problem. Honest."

Obviously the intruder was gone- if there was an intruder. Maybe I was just hearing things. Maybe the bad dreams and the newspaper article had conspired together to spark my imagination.

"Maybe I'm going crazy?" I mumbled as I climbed the open staircase in the lobby that led to the second floor and my office at the end of the long hall.

I sat down at my desk with every intention of working on the never-ending pile of papers that appeared in front of my face daily.

I stared at nothing. My mind was locked into a different position and it wasn't working on the papers.

I felt violated. I felt as though someone was stomping around in my life. I had no idea why I felt that way.

Maybe I should call the sheriff and report what I had seen. Maybe I should stop at that house on my way home from work and do some of my own investigating. Maybe I should forget the whole thing and hope that my mind would let me do so.

"Ellen?"

No answer or sign of acknowledgment came from me.

"Ellen?" repeated Doris in a louder tone.

"What?" I said as I tried to bring myself back into focus.

"Are you all right?"

"Yeah, sure. Why wouldn't I be? I was just thinking about something."

"You sure were. What was it?"

"What was what?"

"This conversation isn't getting us anywhere, Ellen. Here," said Doris as she handed something to me. "This was downstairs on my desk. I'm surprised you didn't see it when you came in."

The envelope wasn't preprinted in the corner with a business return address. The envelope was white and looked like all of those sold at the local dollar stores.

"Who is it from?" asked Doris without trying to hide her curiosity.

"I don't know. I'll look at it later. I need to get busy and print these purchase orders I entered into the computer yesterday afternoon."

"You aren't the least bit curious?"

"No, not at the moment," I answered as I tried to convince Doris with a bold faced lie.

As soon as Doris was out of sight, I ripped open the envelope.

"Oh, my God," I whispered as I gazed at the picture I held in my hand.

I immediately looked at my desk on the corner where I had kept the picture I was holding inside a silver frame.

I knew why I had felt violated earlier.

SAY NOTHING

was printed in bold, black marker across the photograph of my husband as he held our dog and stood next to the cat.

I started shaking with fear, not for myself, but for my husband.

I reached for the telephone and dialed my home number. The ring of the telephone sounded in my ear over and over again.

"Sonny, please pick up the phone. Please be all right," I prayed into the receiver.

"Hello?"

"What took you so long?" I demanded.

"I was outside with the dog. What's wrong?"

"I was worried about you."

"Why? What did you need?"

"I wanted to tell you that I love you. Oh, by the way, have you seen any strangers hanging around the area?"

"No, no, wait a minute. Yeah, I did a few minutes ago. Some guy came to the door looking for someone named Jerry Jenson. You don't know anyone with that name, do you?"

"No. What did the guy look like?'

"What guy?"

"The guy that asked you if you knew Jerry whatever his name was."

"I don't know. I didn't pay much attention to him."

"Why not? You should keep an eye on all strangers. Anything could happen. You know that, don't you?"

"What's this all about?"

"Nothing. It's just the shooting I saw. I guess I'm a little spooked. Did you read the article in the paper about the unidentified dead woman that was found?"

"Yes, but she wasn't found anywhere near here. She's not what you saw."

"I hope you're right. I've got to go, Sonny. Are you feeling okay?'

"Yeah, just a little short of breath but no chest pains."

"Good, I'll talk to you later."

I hung the telephone receiver onto the cradle carefully. I wanted to tell Sonny about the picture but I didn't for fear that the news would upset him so much that he could go right into a heart attack.

I was going to have to deal with this threat on my own.

The rest of the day at work was agonizingly long. I jumped at every sound and snapped at anyone who spoke to me.

When Sonny picked me up at four o'clock, I was so relieved to see him safe and sound that I fought back my tears of joy so he wouldn't have a reason to question me.

I told Sonny nothing about the threat that evening as I kept a smile plastered to my face to hide my fear.

Bedtime came and I fell into a heavy, dreamless sleep even though I thought I would spend a long night of tossing and turning.

The alarm rang the next morning and I had to begin my workday cycle again.

"I'm going out to start the car," said Sonny as he looked at the clock checking to see that he was on schedule.

"No, wait a few more minutes. I'm not going to go in early for the next few days."

"How come?"

"I'm tired of giving them my time. I'll just spend it here with you."

"That sounds good to me."

Sonny and I lingered over coffee until I could linger no longer.

"Let's go, Sonny."

We walked out the front door to a gruesome sight.

Our old, gray cat had been chopped into pieces and dumped onto our sidewalk.

"Sonny, what is that?"

"It's Gray Baby," he said as he gazed at the bloody body parts.

"How can you tell?"

"Look at the ear. See it? It's got the split on the tip of it like Gray Baby's."

"Oh, God, Sonny," I cried, "Who would do this to an old, harmless cat?"

"I don't know, Ellen. I just don't know," he said as tears streamed down his cheeks.

I wiped my eyes as I looked around to see if there were any other messages.

"I'll go get a garbage bag," said Sonny as he turned to go into the house.

I walked to the side of the house and started tugging at the water hose.

Sonny picked up the dead cat and I rinsed the blood from the sidewalk.

He was a big, old, ugly blue gray cat that moved in on my good nature many, many years ago. He brought with him only one eye, an allergy to fleas, and a personality that didn't seem to fit any male tomcat that I ever encountered.

When my family lived in the trailer park, Savage, also known as Gray Baby, was the tiny kitten that was brought home to stay with Natasha, who was my teenage neighbor.

From the first day he was allowed outside, he would visit our house. We watched after him and fed him on occasion when Tasha and her family were away from home for an extended length of time.

The kitten was so comfortable with us that Tasha would have to come knocking on our door to get her little pet.

During his younger tomcat years, Savage got into a fight with another male cat and lost the use of his eye. It had been scratched so severely that Savage had to be taken to a vet. The eye healed but it was never useful again. Savage developed a tendency to turn his head a little to the side so he could focus in on his target with his good eye. The focusing would evolve into an intent stare with the good eye barely blinking.

It was frightening at night to see only one eye reflecting the light in the darkness. The first time I saw the shining one eye through the blackness of night, I didn't know what kind of creature was coming towards me.

In another disagreement with the neighborhood bully, Savage received the punishment of a split ear that eventually healed but made him very identifiable in a crowd of blue gray cats.

In order to keep him out of fights, Savage was neutered and thus became Gray Baby. The name of Savage no longer fit the good natured stay-at-home tomcat that I called Gray Baby.

Tasha's father didn't seem to like the cat and he would kick at him to chase him away. I think Roger's foot connected with Gray Baby's backside once too often and caused the cat some long lasting pain. From that day on, Gray Baby didn't want to go home.

Natasha grew up, married, and left home and Gray Baby. Gray Baby no longer stayed at the trailer after Tasha moved away opting instead to move in on us permanently. He seemed to always keep his one watchful eye open for the return of Tasha.

Checking on the House

A few months after she married, Tasha tried to move Gray Baby to the next county over which was about thirty miles from his original home. Gray Baby didn't like the idea and when he escaped from his new house he stayed hidden for almost a week. Tasha loaded him back into the car and returned him to the trailer park and his home.

Roger and Kathy, Tasha's father and mother, decided to move to South Carolina. They sold the trailer they had been living in to others who moved it out of the trailer park.

That crazy old cat would go and lay down on the ground where the trailer had been set up.

He stopped eating and grieved for his former owners.

It took some powerful persuasion, but we finally got Gray Baby to eat and move back into our home.

That was when I started calling him Bear Kitten. He had the appearance of a grouchy, mean old bear but the demeanor of a gentle kitten.

Bear Kitten was now eighteen years old. He was about as pitiful looking as an old cat can get but he still had a home with us and he was welcome to stay as long as he continued to hang onto the last of his nine lives.

Bear Kitten had shown me that we all can survive with a little help.

When I looked at my ugly, old, blue gray cat, I marveled at his ability to keep going no matter what happened.

I smiled when I saw Bear Kitten. Or at least, I used to.

The world was a much nicer place when I could find a reason to smile.

Bear Kitten died long before I was ready for him to go.

I could have used his services when we lived on Lyons Avenue in a rented house before we got the Habitat

House but I think old age had slowed him down too much. Oh well, we loved him anyway.

"There's that noise again."

"I didn't hear anything."

"Sh-sh-sh ! Don't make a sound," I whispered as I held my index finger straight up in front of my lips.

"I'm not."

I strained to hear it again but it was gone. I knew the noise would be back again.

I had figured out what that annoying sound was but I hadn't seen the source. I had no real visual evidence. The noise would stop as soon as I made a sound so I knew the creature could hear. I was glad to know the varmint had ears.

Since my husband was hard of hearing, I knew he wouldn't believe me if I told him about what it was that I thought I was hearing, not without proof. I had to have proof. The cat was as hard of hearing as Sonny, so he wasn't any help.

My digital clock screamed at me when my eyes focused on the bright red numerals. Two o'clock in the morning and I was wide-awake listening to the noise. It was the very same noise my husband couldn't hear, nor could the cat.

I could hear the scratching and the chewing of the wood. I could almost feel the house scream in pain every time the teeth were sunk into the old wood causing it to splinter and tear.

"I wish it would stop," I whispered.

My mind seemed to amplify the sound. I could hear the scratching and the gnawing and it was driving me crazy.

"It's finally gone," I whispered as I slipped back into slumber.

"Boy, you look terrible," said my worried husband later that same morning.

"I didn't get much sleep because of all the noise that you can't hear," I snapped.

I poured myself a cup of coffee and stood next to the counter trying to focus my mind on the task of beginning a new day.

Suddenly, I saw a brown streak race across the floor.

"Honey, I saw it. I saw the monster that has been eating the house. It's a mouse!" I yelled as I pointed in the direction the brown streak had run.

"You aren't afraid of mice, are you?" he asked sarcastically.

"No, actually I was afraid I was going off the deep end because you weren't able to hear the destruction. I'm glad the creature is real and that I'm not really crazy."

My husband set traps in the kitchen and in my bedroom to catch the creature. I had discovered that the little critter had been living in my sock drawer leaving behind its droppings to cling to every piece of fabric in the drawer.

Night after night the brown mouse would steal the food without springing the traps because my husband had laid the cheese on top of the trigger. Finally, when he forced the cheese down over the trigger, not allowing it to come lose without a tug, we caught the mouse.

"Sonny, I heard the trap spring. Get it out of here, please. I don't want to hear the mouse as it fights to live."

He picked up the trap, loosened the spring, and threw the carcass out the door.

The next night the noise came back.

"Sonny, I must be losing my mind. I heard the scratching and gnawing again last night."

"It must have had a mate. If you catch one mouse, you can bet there will be a second one on the premises."

Two days later we killed the second unwanted visitor.

Now, the only problem we had left to contend with, as far as creepy crawlers were concerned, was the snakes that were using the front and back yard as sun bathing areas before plunging into the creek that was located at the edge of our back yard.

"Sonny, how can we get rid of those snakes?" I asked my husband one day after watching a snake that was about three feet long slither towards my front door.

"I don't know. I don't think we can do anything. The neighbors said they are here every year. This just happens to be a dryer year; therefore, more snakes are going to the water."

"I wouldn't have rented this place if I thought it came with snakes," I mumbled.

In my heart I knew that the next time I heard a strange sound in my wall, I wouldn't think of the harmless little field mouse.

Slithering, multiplying, growing snakes would be what I would know would be living in my walls.

The mere thought of the snakes entering my house was what caused me to pack up bag and baggage and leave. If I had to pick one of life's little surprises, I knew I could tolerate a mouse, but no way were the snakes and I ever going to share the same home.

I wanted to put a sign up in the front yard so the next renter would not be caught by surprise like we were. The sign would read:

BEWARE OF THE SNAKES!!

God, I'm going to miss that ugly, old, gray cat.

"Sonny, go inside and call work for me. Tell them I'm sick and that I'll be in tomorrow."

He made the call while I changed from my work clothes into jeans and a tee shirt.

"I talked to Doris. She said she would tell those who needed to know that you wouldn't be in today."

"Good, we need to talk," I said as I started walking away from the living room. "Wait a second; I'll be right back. I've got to get something from inside my handbag."

When I returned to the room, I handed the torn envelope and the vandalized photograph to my husband.

"Someone knows that I saw the shooting."

"Yeah, but you can't identify anybody," said an excited Sonny.

"They don't know that. Whoever did it thinks I can identify the killer."

"You better go tell the sheriff."

"And take a chance on getting you killed? I can't do that," I said as I fought angry tears.

"What else can we do?" asked a dejected Sonny.

"This guy has been watching me. The reason I stopped going into work early is because I heard someone inside the building and I thought it was Doris. When I called her name and she didn't answer, I knew someone was in there that shouldn't have been. I hid from him so he couldn't find me. But, he found my office and stole my picture of you and our pets that he returned to me with the threat. We need to turn the tables on him but I don't want you hurt, Sonny."

"Don't worry about me."

"I've got to, Sonny. You're all I've got," I whispered softly with all the love I could muster.

"I love you, too."

"Tomorrow morning we'll take the dog with us like we do most of the time anyway. Instead of dropping me off at work, I'm going to let you drive until we get near John's house, then I will slide over and go on my way to work while you and Nikki visit your best friend.

"I want the car so I can take a drive at around ten o'clock to check out some things. You can call me from John's house, but I want you and Nikki to be safe. I don't want John involved in this mess either. You're both too sick to be messing with a mad man."

"Ellen, what are you planning to do?"

"I'm not sure yet. I'll think of something. You keep thinking about this, too. Between the both of us, we should come up with something."

"I'll get John to drive me to…"

"No you won't. Please, Sonny, don't get involved in this. I love you too much to lose you, not like this."

"I'm already involved, Ellen."

"Please, Sonny, stay with John until I come back later today to pick up you and Nikki."

Nikki was about three pounds of tiny creature that demanded all of your love and attention. She was Nikki, our dark brown edged in beige Chihuahua.

My husband, Sonny, and I weren't supposed to be the initial recipients of the pleasure of Nikki's company. She was actually given to Eddy, my oldest son, for companionship.

Eddy felt bad about leaving her alone so much of the time because he worked nights. He started asking us to watch her for him so she wouldn't always be alone.

I worked full time but my husband was disabled and spent a lot of time home alone so he looked forward to the pleasure of Nikki's visits.

Now, Nikki spent all of her time at our house. Eddy decided that she needed a permanent home with us, actually with my husband.

If my husband had to spend time in the hospital, Nikki pouted at me because I believed she thought I had run him off. If I had to be somewhere overnight, she pouted at my husband.

Almost everywhere we went, we took Nikki with us because she was part of the family. If I went to yard sales or flea markets, she was us and in my arms because she would not walk on a leash.

She was full grown when we got her and her timidity was exaggerated. She was afraid of everyone or everything that made a loud noise.

Nikki ran for cover at the hint of a thunderstorm. The clouds thickening up in the sky blotting the sun made her extremely nervous because she recognized the darkness as a pending thunderstorm.

The noise of a vacuum cleaner or a lawnmower was a reason for her to hide.

The raised voices of two people involved in a verbal argument could cause her to hide.

Because Nikki was so sensitive, she had become a source of worry for my husband who needed some place to focus his thoughts and time. Being disabled, Sonny had too much time on his hands and keeping Nikki company and well protected had allowed Sonny to dwell on other problems that weren't his own.

Nikki helped me help my husband who was suffering from a bad heart condition. He had to endure a triple by-pass followed by the placement, at different times, of several stents to hold his veins and arteries open. To complicate his life, he had diabetes and a bad back that had also caused him to endure three surgeries.

Without the need to tend to Nikki, Sonny might have worried himself into an early departure from this world.

Nikki was about ten years old, that was a guess, and had endured the indignity of being spayed. She never was able to have puppies because it was determined that her female workings were too small, but we didn't want the scent of her being in heat to attract a male dog that would harm her.

Her next surgical procedure was for the veterinarian to remove two broken teeth that were being held in her mouth by skin only. The broken teeth would flop around in her mouth and prevent her from eating.

A couple of months later we discovered a growth on her belly which was diagnosed as breast cancer and the tumor was removed by the same vet that removed the teeth.

Nikki had required a lot of worry and loving care.

Nikki had been enduring the indignities of growing old but then, so had we.

We would keep Nikki with us as long as humanly possible and prayed that we all three- Nikki, Sonny, and Ellen (that was me) grow older with the pleasure of each other's company.

Sonny shrugged his shoulders. I accepted the shrug as acknowledgement that he and Nikki would stay at John's house and be safe.

What was I going to do? I was going to do exactly what got me into trouble in the first place. I was going to do some snooping.

"Doris, I've got an errand to run. I'll be back in a little while," I said as I left the school board office. I had breezed past Doris quickly because I didn't want to have to answer any questions to explain the purpose of my errand.

Into the car I climbed. Once the car door was closed, I took a deep breath as I held my eyes closed. I had to clear all the clutter from the cracks and crevices of my mind's eye so I could concentrate on what was ahead.

"Ellen, what are you going to do?" I asked myself in a loud, angry voice as I started the car.

Slowly I drove my car from the parking lot. I turned onto the street that would lead me to what I hoped would be some answers.

The house that had caused my problems was ahead on the left.

"Don't slow down, Dummy. Don't let anyone think you're interested in it at all."

I glanced out the car window to see that the house was closed up tight. The shades were drawn and there was no sign of life.

"What can I do?' I mumbled.

The wooded area was beside me. I had seen a partial roadway that had been made by some type of vehicle plowing through the weeds. That's what I was going to do. I was going to drive off the street onto the makeshift road as far as I could go without getting my car stuck.

I drove past the wooded area onto a private driveway where I turned my vehicle around facing the direction from which I had driven. At the edge of the wooded area I traveled onto a nonexistent road that led through the weeds and trees that were next to the house I needed to investigate.

The car bounced and jumped across the rough terrain. The tall weeds smacked and slapped at the sides of the car but I kept going until I drove to a clearing of sorts. The area looked as if someone had cut down trees and weeds and was planning to build a house nestled in the woods far enough from the street to make the inhabitants feel like they were living an isolated existence in the country with no nearby neighbors and no distractions.

I looked around, peering through the windshield of my car. I saw nothing that would discourage me from exiting the car if you don't count the utter loneliness that surrounded me.

I automatically reached for the lock but stopped my hand before I pressed the button. I might need to make a fast exit and I didn't want to have to struggle with trying to fit the key into the lock when I was scared out of my mind.

I placed the key ring holding the ignition key around my ring finger so I wouldn't lose it. I wouldn't have to struggle with trying to find it when my life depended on it.

I had already changed my shoes before I left work. I made sure I was wearing reasonable, flat-heeled shoes that were good for running if that became necessary.

I was scared and nervous because I didn't know what I was going to confront. I hoped my only confrontation would be with an empty house.

I gently closed the car door. I wanted no telltale sound to announce my arrival.

I bent my body slightly forward trying to force my body into a position of flight because I definitely was not going to fight.

I crept slowly through the brush until I saw the house. Again, I saw no shadowy signs of life, no kind of activity that might force me to turn around and run back to my car.

I paused time after time listening, straining to hear any sounds of discouragement. I was looking for a reason, any reason, to run.

The closer I got to the house, the louder my heart pounded in my chest. I had to quiet my own noise so I closed my eyes momentarily while I took a deep breath.

When I opened my eyes, my heart pounding had silenced and I moved closer and closer to the house.

The wooded area ran along the side and the back of the house. I had some protection from being seen from the house or the street. At least I wasn't trying to cross an open field.

There was no barrier of any kind such as a fence or wall to scale and cross. There was no vehicle parked in the driveway.

I tried to look in a side window but I was too short. I walked to the back door where there was a small window inset in the door but it was completely covered by what looked like a towel. A window that was positioned off to the side of the door was also covered with something other than a curtain, a sheet perhaps.

I stood quietly near the back door and listened. I heard no activity, no movement of any kind. I decided to turn the doorknob just to see what would happen.

It turned.

I was not expecting to be able to go inside the house.

"What should I do?" I prayed as I pushed the door open.

When I went from the bright outdoor light into the subdued, curtained interior of the house, I was blinded for a moment until my eyes adjusted to the drastic change.

I entered the kitchen that was remarkably clean, almost too clean.

A few steps further into the house led me past what looked like an empty bedroom into the living room where I knew I saw the shooting.

I looked from one side of the room to the other side trying to find a clue.

The room was not in a shambles from any kind of a struggle. Everything appeared to be in its proper place and the smell of cleaning products filled the air.

I walked to the spot where the body fell. I stooped and touched the carpet with my hand. The carpet was wet.

"He's cleaned up the blood," I whispered as I straightened up so I could get out of there.

"Who is this guy?"

I started looking for something with a name on it. I thought about the mailbox. I looked out the front window and saw no one, not even a passing car on the road. I unlocked the front door and stepped outside far enough and long enough to reach my hand inside the mailbox that was attached to the front of the house.

There was a small postcard in the box. I snatched it from the box and quickly closed and locked the front door.

The name on the card that was a water bill was Dale Thompson.

I kept the card. I wanted to remember that name always. I stuffed it deep into my pocket so I couldn't possibly lose it.

I retraced my steps until I got to the kitchen where I heard a noise.

"Oh, God, he's coming in here," I whispered as I looked for a place to run.

The bedroom was the only place I could go. There had to be a closet or a bathroom where I could duck out of sight until I could figure out my next move.

The bedroom was as clean and sparkly as the living room and kitchen. There was a closet and a door that led to the bathroom. I opened the closet door and climbed inside, ducking behind the clothes that were on hangers.

The back door opened and I heard a voice.

"Come out now, Ellen," growled the man as he stomped through his house.

I cringed lower in the closet. I placed my hand on the floor and felt a blanket that I pulled over myself to try to hide even more.

I willed myself to breathe slowly, quietly, and not to make a single move.

"I know you're here. I followed you."

The closet door flew open and I could hear the rapid heavy breathing of an angry man. I knew my life was dwindling down to seconds. Suddenly the blanket was pulled from me and I was totally exposed.

The man laughed, a maniacal sound that gave me the sense that I was facing a crazy man. I braced my feet and pushed my back against the wall.

A hand pushed through the hanging clothes toward my head. I ducked and rolled a little to the side.

"Get out of there, now," growled the menacing figure standing over me.

I rolled my body back and forth just out of his reach.

He took a step forward and grabbed me by the back of my shirt. He jerked me out of the closet and onto my feet.

"You nosey, no good…." he sputtered at me.

"Why are you after me?" I screamed. "What did I ever do to you?"

"You haven't done anything to me yet, but you could. I can't take that chance," he answered as he held me in a chokehold.

"I've never seen you before today, right now. What can I do to you?"

"Don't lie to me, Ellen," he whispered angrily into my ear. "You saw me. You saw what I did. You saw me shoot that woman. You saw me do it. I saw you looking in my window. I saw you looking at me," he said as he squeezed tighter with his chokehold.

"I didn't see who shot that person. I didn't even know it was a woman until you said so. I didn't know for sure if it what I saw was real. All I saw was the flash of the gun and the falling body. I swear I never saw you."

"It's too late now, Ellen. I can't let you leave now," he said as he started pushing me forward.

"How do you know who I am? How did you find me?"

"You drive past this house at least twice a day. Those stupid people at your office placed your name on your office door. All I had to do was follow you. I've done that many times. I'm pretty good at following people. You never saw me follow you, did you?"

"No, I didn't. Are you going to kill me, too? Are you going to dump my body on Trash Dump Road?"

"I have no choice. I don't need any loose ends, any witnesses."

I felt the hard barrel of a handgun pushing against my lower back as the man held me with his arm around my throat while his other hand shoved the gun into my back.

"Who are you?" I asked in a barely audible whisper.

"I'm the man who is going to kill you. It doesn't matter what my name is, does it?"

"I guess not. I'd just like to know your name before I die."

"Dale Thompson."

"What was the woman's name? The one you killed?" I continued to whisper. I was trying to buy some time. I wanted to find a way to live.

"She told me her name was Bonnie Simpson. I picked her up in a bar a couple of hundred miles from here and brought her to this place to have a little fun. When I was finished with her, I had to get rid of her. I thought the dump was appropriate for that poor white trashy female."

"Is that what you're going to do to me?"

"I'm going to skip the fun part. I only want to get rid of you."

He guided me to the back door that he had left standing open and shoved me through it telling me to walk into the wooded area to my car.

I was too afraid to do anything except what he said. I had no idea how I was going to get away from him in one piece. I was truly sorry that my husband wasn't with me.

He pushed me harder with the gun gouging my lower back.

"Get moving or I'll shoot you right here."

"Okay, okay," I cried as my mind churned trying to find a solution.

When I reached the corner of the house, I went limp causing him to lose his grip on my throat. I fell forward to the ground and an oxygen tank crashed over Dale Thompson's head. The gun went off sending a bullet into a nearby tree.

I scrambled away from my enemy and watched him fall into a huge heap of flesh on the ground where I had been lying seconds earlier.

"Where did you come from?"

"Someone had to watch your back."

"Sonny, I don't know how to thank you."

"We'll discuss that later. Now, go call the police, Ellen. John and I will watch this sucker and if he moves, I'll shoot him."

I raced to a neighbor's house and pleaded with the little, old lady who answered the door to call the police.

When I returned to help my husband, I saw John, Sonny's best friend, struggling with the oxygen tank trying to get it back into working order so he could use the life sustaining oxygen it contained. He never went anywhere without the heavy tank.

Nikki, my beloved pet Chihuahua was following me and shaking so badly that I had no choice but to pick her up and carry her.

I smiled when I realized that my husband who was suffering with a chronic heart condition and John Carson who was trying of outlive the terminal effects of emphysema, had saved my life. Thankfully, Sonny had not done as I had instructed him to do.

I looked up to the sky offering a prayerful thank you.

CHAPTER 11
UNFRIENDLY BETRAYAL

I was getting good at near misses with my life and livelihood. I actually forced myself to join the computer generation. I also learned that friendship is not always as it seems.

I stared at the brightly lit screen in front of me. I didn't move a muscle. Only my mind was capable of working and it seemed to be spinning at warp speed.

I read those ugly words over and over again.

There is a thief among us who is from the north.

No one in the office had any known ties to the northern part of the country except me. Even though I was born a Virginia, in Charlottesville to be specific, the derogatory name of "Yankee" had been hurled in my direction many times by my coworkers.

I sounded like a northerner because I was raised in Ohio from the age of two to adulthood. I did not return to Virginia, my roots, until I was in my late thirties; but, of course, by that time I had reached the age where I had no trace of my southern heritage in my speech pattern.

Even though I had tried to change on many different occasions when the pain of being ostracized was felt by me, I could not make myself sound like a native Virginian.

I enunciated my words too clearly. I spoke my words in what was considered an abrupt tone. I expressed my thoughts in short bursts that were clear, concise, and went directly to the point.

I knew the e-mail plastered on the bulletin board operated by a local politician's wife was aimed directly at me.

But, why me? Who hated me that much?

I forced my fingers to move to the computer mouse so I could scroll further into the bulletin board to see if there were more messages posted that were aimed at me.

Nothing was there. No other life destroying threats were posted for my frightened eyes to see.

What if my boss got wind of this? Would he believe it?

I had always thought a computer was a wonderful invention until that day, that point in time, when I realized what a negative force it had become to me.

Of course, I didn't expect to use a computer for anything other than a tool and I hadn't until the creation of the Internet, which brought along with it the gossip-mongering bulletin boards.

Not all bulletin boards held life-destroying messages. Some were used for gathering of useful information related to careers or hobbies.

The bulletin board I was looking at was the replacement for the beauty parlor, the backyard fence, or the local diner where people gathered to talk about their neighbors and so-called friends.

Spreading rumors by word of mouth could be just as destructive as a bulletin board but it took a lot longer to do. Perhaps along the word of mouth gossip line the truth could be interjected and the rumor could die a nasty death.

That didn't happen with bulletin boards.

The words of a bulletin board were fast and efficient at destroying a business, a career, and a life. All people with access to a computer could see the words flash before them. Most computerites, in my small town, would accept those destructive innuendoes as gospel, making sure that the poor unfortunates who didn't have access to seeing the words before them were told by a friend or relative or the words were printed in black and white for them to read.

Whenever I glanced at this bulletin board, which wasn't very often, I wanted to post a message telling the system operator to get a life. Monitoring and editing an active bulletin board was time consuming requiring a lot of butt-in-the-chair time with a pair of eyes glued to the computer screen.

I turned off the monitor and shut down the computer. I didn't want to see its destructive light again. All I wanted to do was go to bed and sleep so I could wake up the next morning refreshed. I wanted to believe that this was all a dream, a nightmare, and that my life would continue on without interruption.

I tossed and turned dreaming about a gigantic computer that was controlling me with its giant keyboard. No one was pressing the keys. They were being pulled down from beneath or inside the keyboard spelling out the tasks and tortures to be administered to me. All of the instructions were coming from within the computer.

The giant monitor screen seemed to sway as if dancing to some strange rhythmic music and the monitor had a face with a haughty grin.

The monitor was bobbing and weaving with the keyboard merrily spelling out my future.

…stealing which causes one to lose a job…lose one's home…lose one's family…lose one's income…lose one's hospitalization…lose one's car…lose one's life…

I woke up covered with sweat with my heart beating so fast that I thought it would pound its way out of my chest.

I took deep calming breaths telling myself that it was a bad dream.

I jumped out of bed and ran to the bathroom where I washed the sweat from my face. I looked into the mirror and I could see the dancing computer in the background hovering over my reflection as it did its bobbing and weaving dance.

I closed my eyes tightly as I stood in front of the mirror.

"Please God, let it be gone," I prayed.

I opened my eyes and it was gone.

I threw cold water onto my face to make sure I was completely awake.

I didn't want to dream anymore so I was not going to go back to sleep. It was two in the morning, which was about three and a half hours earlier than the time for which my alarm clock was set.

I went to my computer and turned it on to power it up so I could see if the trash talk was still there.

The internet took me to the bulletin board where I spotted a second entry.

Check the desk of the one with ties to the north... Proof is there.................................
What proof? It can't be talking about me!

I checked to see what name had been assigned to the posting. It was signed "Unfriendly."

I searched through every part, every message, every reply, everything I could read to see if I might be able to spot anything that would tell me or just give me a hint about who "unfriendly" was.

Screen after screen produced no results, nothing that would indicate who my opponent might be.

When I arrived at the office, I tried to sneak in without speaking to anyone. I didn't want to look into the faces of my coworkers and see the doubt etched into their brows.

I held my head down, staring at my feet, as I walked in behind two other ladies who hadn't seen or, at least, hadn't verbally acknowledged my presence.

"Ellen, Mr. Houston wants to see you right away," came a shout from within the lobby.

I stopped walking and felt my knees begin to buckle. I jerked myself into a stiff-legged position to keep from falling onto the floor from embarrassment.

I turned around to see who had shouted at me. It was Nancy, Mr. Houston's secretary. She was waving and yelling at me to make sure I had heard her previous shouted order.

I nodded and continued walking after I forced my legs to unlock. I needed to get rid of everything I was carrying before I stepped into Mr. Houston's office. I needed to collect my thoughts so I could plan a line of defense against the ugly innuendoes on the bulletin board.

I forced myself to hold my head up high with my shoulders back and a smile plastered firmly across my face.

"Ellen, there has been an accusation made that you are a thief and I called you in here so we could get to the bottom of the problem. There has been some money taken and a finger has been pointed at you. Do you know anything about this missing money?" he asked slowly with no indication that he believed I was the thief.

"What money? How much? Who is accusing me? Why?" I sputtered rapidly without expecting any answers.

I took a deep breath to ward off the tears.

"God, don't let me cry," I prayed.

Of course I was going to cry. I always cried when I was angry beyond words. I was prepared, though. I had shoved a couple of tissues inside my skirt pocket in case of an emergency.

"It was a tidy sum of money collected for the retirement gift for Barbara Shortt. It was left in Nancy's office hidden in a desk drawer that was locked. Now the money is missing. Nancy isn't accusing you. She actually thought one of the cleaning people had taken it."

"Then why are you asking me?"

"Because of an e-mail I received. I need to search your desk, but I want you to be present while I do the looking."

"Sure, but you're not going to find anything. I didn't take the money," I cried as I dabbed at my eyes with the tissue.

"I'm sorry about this."

"Who was the e-mail from, Mr. Houston?"

"It was anonymous. I don't have any idea who it came from."

"Did they mention my name?"

"No, not specifically."

"Then how do you know it was me the e-mail was written about?"

"I just do, Ellen."

Of course, he found nothing incriminating. There wasn't anything to find, not in my desk.

The day was endless and the looks and glances I received from people told me that everyone knew what had taken place.

I drove home and upon entering my house, I went directly to the computer to see if there was another installment of the destruction of my life.

It was there, installment number three.

You checked the wrong desk... try the one at home. Remember the ties to the north............

The only desk I had at home was the one I had my computer sitting on.

Maybe they weren't referring to me. Maybe the north could mean Bluefield, West Virginia, not Ohio. Maybe I was reading too much into the word north.

If that were the case, just about anyone in the office could be accused of stealing. Most everybody had family ties with people to the north of Stillwell, Virginia.

Now they can see that it wasn't just me that was being accused. It could have been anybody in that office. Not me. I didn't do it.

My mind and heart wanted to accept my perfectly logical and rational explanation as the truth.

Everyone has to be able to see, just like I can, that I'm not the only person who could be guilty of theft.

The next workday was no better than the previous one. Either my coworkers weren't aware of the third posting or they were convinced I was guilty.

"Lynn," I whispered to a lady whom I thought was a friend, "what has everybody been saying about the trash talk that was posted on the bulletin board?"

"I haven't heard a thing, Ellen. I don't know what you're talking about," she said sweetly as she smiled at me.

"Forget it, Lynn. I've got to get back to work," I said as I slowly walked away from someone I had considered a friend.

I guess it isn't to her advantage career wise to be seen talking with an accused thief.

I could see my future as told by my nightmarish computer. I was going to lose everything that ever meant anything to me because of a few lines typed into a computer by someone who was trying to lead the powers-that-be to the guilty party. I happened to get in the way. At least, I hoped that was the reason. I hoped I wasn't a direct target.

I was the only person in the whole office who was openly having money problems.

I had a husband with a chronic illness. His medical and prescription expenses were consuming any extra money I may have had. I begged for extra projects or jobs that would pay me extra money beyond my regular salary.

But, I didn't steal that money. I'm not that stupid, I thought as I pondered who could be the real thief.

I entered the internet world from my computer at my workstation. Now my antagonizer was talking to the guilty party directly.

Dear Ties to the North
A new car is expensive. How did you do it?
Unfriendly

"It's called credit, Stupid. How do you think any major item is bought in this day and time?" I mumbled in response to the posting.

Of course, I had a new car and I had an enormous debt. The car I had been driving literally fell apart while I was driving it. I had no choice. I had to have another car.

We lived in a rural area where no public transportation was available. To get from point A to point B, you had to have a vehicle.

Who else bought a new car? I'm sure somebody else in this whole place of business bought a new car recently. But who?

At mid-morning during a short break from work, I scoured the parking lot looking for new vehicles.

They were all new. At least they looked new to me since I wasn't a car aficionado.

I had yet to see a reference to the gender of the thief. Maybe it was a man with ties to the north? Again, that could be any of many different males.

All of my coworkers were avoiding me except Diana whom I hoped would remain my steadfast friend. She hadn't been involved with any of the snubbing by my coworkers or the whispers shielded by the hands. She had been on vacation. I certainly wished she were back at the office so I could have a friend to talk to. I really needed a friend.

Unless someone called Diana to fill her in on what was happening when she arrived home from her trip to visit family out of state, she was unlikely to know what was happening. She wouldn't know that I was being targeted as the "Yankee" with "ties to the north."

I was sure Diana hadn't been surfing the internet because she didn't have a computer at home and her terminal at work hadn't been connected to the internet.

I needed to talk to a friendly face. I needed to know that I had an ally. That friendly face and ally wouldn't be at work until the next day.

When I left work to go home, I walked past people who turned their heads away from me to avoid looking at me.

Upon arriving home, I went directly to my computer to discover what new nail for my coffin had been driven into place.

> **Dear Ties to the North**
> **Confess! It's good for the**
> **soul.........................**
> **Unfriendly**

"Confess to what? It's not me, everybody. I don't have anything to confess to. Get a life and leave me alone," I shouted at the computer screen.

My home telephone no longer rang with cheery greetings from friends. My husband didn't know what to do to help me and due to his chronic heart condition, I didn't want to let him know how serious this situation was becoming.

I forced myself to go to bed hoping and praying that the nightmare computer wouldn't return to haunt me.

My not being able to sleep could have been caused by my suffering from the throes of guilt, but that wasn't the case. My mind kept searching through the names and faces of people I knew in this small town. My mind was looking for a reason, any reason, why anyone would do this to me.

I rose from my bed unable to sleep, unable to rest, unable to pinpoint my enemy.

I went to my computer again.

Dear Ties to the North
Where is the money?
Unfriendly

It wasn't going to stop.

I entered the inner sanctum of the bulletin board world and posted my own message to Unfriendly. I had to have some answers.

Dear Unfriendly
Where do you work? Who are you after?
Interested Party

I pressed the send key and remained in front of my monitor waiting for a reply.

Dear Interested Party
Why are you interested?
Unfriendly

My enemy must have been sitting in front of the computer, just like I was.

Dear Unfriendly
I'm being accused and I'm not guilty.
Interested Party

My response left no doubt it was me my accuser was after.

Dear Interested Party
Life sucks.
Unfriendly

I countered with agreement.

Dear Unfriendly
It sure does.
Interested Party

I scrolled through the bulletin board chatter again searching for a hint, a sign that would lead me to the revelation of my accuser. E-mail after e-mail was flashed on my screen, yet nothing helped.

Mr. Houston summoned me to his office later that morning.

"Ellen, I'm sorry to have to tell you this, but I'm going to have to suspend your employment without pay."

"Why? I didn't steal that money!" I shouted angrily.

"Too many fingers are pointing in your direction. Too many coincidences that can't be explained to anyone's satisfaction are cropping up," he explained sadly. "Several of your coworkers are refusing to work with you until the matter is cleared up."

"I didn't do it, Mr. Houston. No names have ever been used on the internet accusation. How can you pinpoint me as the thief?"

"You recently deposited an amount of money equal to what is missing in your checking account. Where did that money come from?"

"I borrowed it to use as a down payment for the car I needed to get back and forth to work. How did you know about that deposit? How did you get personal, private information about my checking account?"

"This is a small town, Ellen. Information can he had if you know the right person."

"There is no way I would know how much money was collected. And think about it, Mr. Houston, please think about it. Do you honestly think I would be stupid enough to deposit the exact amount that was taken if I had stolen that money? Do you think I'm that stupid?" I said as my voice was rising in pitch with each angry word.

"Control yourself, Ellen. Getting angry with me isn't going to help."

"What is going to help me, Mr. Houston? I didn't steal that money. How can I make you believe me? How can I make the people I work with who are supposed to be my friends believe me? Who is my accuser, Mr. Houston? How can you believe an accusation from someone who won't identify himself or herself?" I asked loudly.

"Calm down, Ellen."

"No, I can't calm down, I want you to answer my questions."

"I can't."

"You can't? Or you won't? Which is it?"

"I can't. I don't know who the person is."

I looked at Mr. Houston and saw him shrink before my eyes. The boss I had admired and to whom I had been loyal, in truth, was a very small person.

"I'll take my vacation now. You don't have to suspend me. I've got thirty-three days of accumulated vacation days. I'll use that to find out who is doing this to me."

"Good, Ellen, that's what I hoped you would say," said Mr. Houston as he stood up behind his desk, which was a signal to let me know that the meeting was over and that I should leave.

"Mr. Houston, there is one more thing I need to know. The internet accuser has never said whether the thief was male or female, or whether the thief worked at this perfect place of employment, or what money was stolen. How come everyone has arrived at my name? Is it because I'm from the north? Is that what you think? Look at my application someday and check out where I was born. You might be a little surprised. Everyone pointing fingers might be a little surprised," I said as I walked out his door closing it behind me. I was holding my head high and smiling as I walked to my office to gather my belongings to start my vacation. I was going to find out why this was happening to me.

I knew most of my information about what was happening to me was going to have to come from the disreputable, evil machine that was the vehicle being used to tarnish my name.

Diana would help me by keeping tabs on what was happening at the office. I had no worries about her help. I knew I could count on her. She was my only true friend.

My income would continue for a while because I was taking vacation days in lieu of suspension, but that wouldn't last forever.

Even though I walked out of the office with a smile on my face, I was crying inside.

I had always been an outsider in this town.

I was born in Charlottesville but my roots were in Richard County, twenty miles from this small town. My mother was a Richard County native and I still had an uncle living at the old home place.

Through inheritance, I would eventually become a landowner in Richard County. My great grandmother left the property to her grandchildren. My mother was one of those three grandchildren. When my mother died, I was in line for the real estate. Wasn't that ironic? I really wasn't an outsider. I had roots.

Am I still an outsider because I sound different?

My family which consisted of my husband and two sons were not welcomed with outstretched arms when we arrived fifteen years ago, and I'm sorry to say, the residents of this small town are no friendlier today than when we arrived.

I planted myself in front of my computer, connected to the internet, which hooked me into the bulletin board where I planned to stay until I was satisfied with the answers I was looking for. I wanted to know who was doing this and why?

Dear Unfriendly
What's happening?
Interested Party

Now, I would wait.

It was ten o'clock in the morning when I rose from my chair and cleaned house. I vacuumed, dusted, washed, ironed, and generally drove my husband crazy with all the noise and odors associated with cleaners.

I was never more the five minutes away from the computer screen as I awaited a response.

No response was forthcoming during my or my accuser's normal working hours of eight to four thirty.

My accuser had a day job.

At five thirty there was a response.

> **Dear Interested Party**
> **The thief is still free but the authorities**
> **are closing in. Soon the truth will win…**
> **Unfriendly**

Nothing specific was said that I could grab onto and run with to help clear my name.

> **Dear Unfriendly**
> **What is the truth?**
> **Interested Party**

I knew I wasn't going to get a response to that question, but I had to try.

Before I went to bed I decided to send another message.

> **Dear Unfriendly**
> **Nobody's going to catch me.**
> **Interested Party**

I went to bed with a smile on my face. If that posting didn't get a reaction, nothing would.

Well, the only reaction I was aware of was silence. Unfriendly went underground and no more postings were made by Unfriendly for three days. That is unless Unfriendly was using a different name. If so, I wasn't able to detect it.

> **Dear Unfriendly**
> **Ha! Ha!**
> **Interested Party**

That was my first posting to the bulletin board after the bragging message that stated that no one was going to catch me.

Dear Unfriendly
Cat got your tongue?
Interested Party
I was trying my best to force the issue.
Dear Unfriendly
It was you, wasn't it?
Interested Party
A few hours later I posted another knife in the ribs.
Dear Unfriendly
Do you need bail money?
Interested party
I knew if these messages had been sent to me and not from me, I would be angry, very angry.

I called Diana to do some snooping about what was happening at the office.

"How's everything going?" I asked cheerfully.

"Fine. When are you coming back to work?"

"Maybe never if I don't find out who is trying to crucify me. Do you have any ideas?" I probed.

"What are you talking about?" asked Diana with a tone of voice that had a twinge of insincerity.

"You've got to know, Diana. I'm sure each and every coworker of mine and yours were dying to tell you the tale of the firing of Ellen, the thief."

"No, tell me what this is all about. I don't know anything about it. Whose money were you supposed to have stolen?"

"The money for the retirement gift for Barbara Shortt. They think I stole it."

"You wouldn't do that."

"Do you know anyone that hates me that much, Diana?"

"No, none, not a soul, I can't think of anyone who would do this to you. I wouldn't be able to hazard a guess. Susan has been told to do all your work and boy is she steamed."

"Why Susan?"

"I don't know except that Mr. Houston told her she had to do it until you came back to work."

"No wonder she's steamed. I may never get back to work."

"I've been busy trying to catch up on all the work that piled up while I was on vacation."

"Everybody there knows you're my best friend. Has anybody given you a hard time?"

"No, no one."

"Oh, okay. I'd better go before I get you into trouble for talking on the phone to an almost convicted felon. Call me when you get home, will you?" I asked as I hung up the telephone with a puzzled look on my face.

She didn't sound or act like my best friend, Diana. I wondered why there was a difference in her voice and actions. Also, I wondered why she wasn't feeling any antagonism from her coworkers because she was my best friend. I knew what those ladies were like and I knew what they would do. Treating Diana as if nothing was wrong was not one of them. That is unless she had joined their forces.

Another annoying tidbit of worry surfaced when I thought about what Diana had said about the stolen money. Diana indicated that she knew nothing about what was going on with regard to my suspension from work, yet she knew that the stolen item in question was money.

I went through her conversation in my mind and was sure Diana had mentioned the missing money first.

If she didn't know that was happening, how did she know about the money?

"No, it's not Diana. Diana is my friend, my best friend, my only friend," I mumbled softly.

I didn't want to find out that I was wrong about my loyalty to Diana.

Seeds of doubt had been planted and were rapidly growing filling in the holes in my mind.

I started playing around with e-mail addresses.

First, I sent Nancy a message about a file I had on my desk. It needed some attention so she should take it to Mr. Houston to see what he wanted to do.

Next, I sent an e-mail to the personnel secretary to make sure she knew I was on paid vacation.

The third message used an e-mail address that I thought would belong to Diana if she had a computer at home.

Dear Diana
When did you get a computer?
Ellen

I pressed the send button and specified that I wanted to be notified of receipt. When I checked a few hours later, the receipt was posted. Diana had received my message.

I never received an e-mail from Diana signed with her given name, but I had received many messages from her under the pseudonym of Unfriendly.

Diana, my best friend in all the world and in all of this small town, was my accuser.

Why?

I tried to call Diana at home but the telephone kept ringing with no one picking up the receiver.

I composed an e-mail and sent it across the internet.

Diana
Why did you do this to me?
Ellen

There were tears in my eyes when I was puzzling out the truth that Diana was my enemy. I wasn't sure if the tears were from being angry about the actions of my best friend or from the sadness of discovering that I no longer had a best friend.

A few moments passed allowing Diana to compose her response.

Ellen
Because you don't belong here.
Diana

I tried to e-mail Diana several more times but I received no response.

It was as though "Unfriendly" Diana had disappeared into her own ugly world leaving me to explain what had happened when I had no idea what the answer was.

Mr. Houston told me the rest of the story.

"Ellen, Diana came into work this morning and handed in her resignation citing personal problems as her reason for leaving. When I asked her about trying to destroy you, her best friend, her response was that you're an outsider. She said you don't belong here. You're not family.

"She told me she used the missing money to pay some bills. She asked me to deduct the amount from her last paycheck that she was to receive. She begged me not to prosecute which I agreed to do."

"Would you have prosecuted me?"

"I can't answer that."

"I can."

"Ellen, you can come back to work tomorrow morning."

"No thank you. I'm going to finish using the remainder of my paid vacation days and then I'm going to find a better place to work."

"Are you sure that's what you want to do?"

"I'm positive. I do want you to write me a glowing letter of recommendation and if I ever hear of you uttering a derogatory word about my employment with you, I know how to start a smear campaign. Do you get my drift?"

"No problem, Ellen. You've always been an excellent employee."

I wouldn't start a smear campaign against Mr. Houston. I wouldn't want to put anyone else through what had been done to me.

All I wanted was a letter of recommendation to use in my search for a new job, a new life, and hopefully a new best friend.

I think I'll stake a claim on the family home place and start over in Richard County.

"Move over, Uncle Jim. Here I come."

CHAPTER 12
THE YARD SALE

I had real trouble when it came to keeping a best friend…

Every Saturday morning I rose from my bed to embark on my quest to find what was lost from my life.

I made it a point to be home in the spring, summer, and early fall, each Saturday morning, so I could visit every yard sale I could find in my neighborhood and the surrounding neighborhoods until I could find no more sales that day.

I rarely bought anything but I looked at everything the sellers had to offer.

"Are you looking for anything in particular?" asked many of the sellers.

"No," I would answer as I shook my head from side to side.

I continued to open boxes and peer inside them searching for my lost secret.

I dressed myself in old attire that would be appropriate for yard sales. Blue jeans and tee shirts were what I regularly wore. I really couldn't dress much better than that because I couldn't afford it. Most of my clothing was purchased at yard sales along with the furnishings in my home.

I worked as a bartender in a dark, dingy bar in the downtown Cleveland area. It wasn't in the center of town. It was off to the side near an industrialized area where most of the bar patrons were white-skinned, blue-collar workers who were just barely getting by, too.

The tips in the bar were small and my working hours were short, but it was the best I could do until I got back what was rightfully mine.

I wanted to move on to find a better life but I couldn't. I had to keep looking. My friends and family thought I was obsessed. Maybe I was. I had to find my stolen inheritance. I knew I would find it. It wouldn't stay hidden in this city forever.

I looked every Saturday. I couldn't look any other day because I worked, but my Saturdays were reserved for looking.

"Do you have any jewelry boxes for sale or maybe some old necklaces and rings?" I started asking just in case they hadn't placed everything they were planning to sell on display.

The item I was looking for was a necklace that had been stolen two years earlier. It was a double strand of pearls that my father had given my grandmother when he first went to work for a living. He had put a down payment on the pearl necklace when he received his first payday and had paid on it every week for six months.

The pearl necklace didn't cost a lot by today's standards, but the fifty dollars he paid fifty years ago made the value of the necklace much more noteworthy.

I didn't think the pearls were real when I first received the necklace from my Aunt Mintha at the bequest of my grandmother.

I had been comparing them to a strand of fake pearls and had noticed an enormous weight difference between the two necklaces. I had thought the feather light strand of beads was fake not realizing that real pearls were much lighter than the fakes. I knew the people who stole the pearls didn't know their value. I had never told Teresa that the pearls were real so I knew the pearls were taken by accident. They were hidden in a secret compartment in my jewelry box. There were many other glittery items that Teresa would have thought were valuable.

In truth, the jewelry box contained lots of shiny, costume jewelry most of which was available at a discount or dollar store. The only thing of value was my gold ring representing good old Lincoln High School. My high school ring held lots of sentimental value and some material value but not much. The pearl necklace was valuable both ways but the most important value to me was sentimental because it was tied to both my grandmother and my father.

It was hard for me to believe that Teresa would steal from me. I thought Teresa was my friend, my only real friend. I had learned not to trust those around me in this large city.

We had a lot in common, Teresa and me. I was a lonely fat woman with two children and Teresa was a lonely fat woman with two children. I was divorced but Teresa was married to a chronic lazy man who didn't want to work for a living. He thought society owed him something. Why he felt that way was a question for which I never discovered an answer.

"Teresa, I'm going to take the kids to visit their grandparents in southern Ohio," I said cheerfully one evening as I was packing a couple of raggedy old suitcases with faded tee shirts and well-worn shorts for my sons to wear during the visit.

"How long will you be gone?" Teresa asked innocently.

"I'm leaving Friday evening after I get home from work and I'll be back Sunday evening. Would you watch my house for me?" I asked excitedly.

"Sure, no problem. I'll be home all weekend."

"I think there's been someone prowling around inside my house when I'm gone. Things have been moved and are not always where I last saw them. I really can't explain it. Maybe I'm just getting paranoid living in this city with no man around the house. Have you ever seen anyone around here that doesn't belong here?" I asked worriedly.

"No, Ellen, I can't say that I have. Maybe one of the kids moved the stuff you're talking about?"

"Maybe. I don't know. It's just a feeling that I have. Keep an eye out, okay? I'll stop by with some of the baby-sitting money before I leave. I'll give you half before I go and I'll give you the rest of it when I get back. Okay?"

"Can't I have it all now?"

"No, I need to have a little extra in case I run into car trouble or something, which I shouldn't. Sunday or Monday is the best I can do. I need to go get some change but I'll bring it to your house before I leave. Okay?" I explained earnestly so Teresa wouldn't think I was trying to cheat her.

"I guess that will have to do," said Teresa as she let the screen door bang when she left my house.

I loaded my excited sons into the car as soon as I arrived home from work. I made a quick stop at Teresa's house, which was directly in front of my own house, and gave Teresa twenty-five dollars. I saw no sign of Bobby so maybe Teresa could keep the money herself.

"You're sure you won't be back until Sunday?" asked Teresa.

"Yes, why?"

"Just checking. I want to make sure I watch the place," answered Teresa as she smiled sweetly.

I discovered, much to my dismay, Teresa was glad to see me leaving, finally. She had a lot to do and she wanted to get started as soon as possible. But, she would wait until the next morning to be sure I wasn't going to turn around and come right back home. She definitely didn't want me to come back and discover what she and Bobby were going to be doing before they had a chance to finish the job.

Bright and early Saturday morning while I was having breakfast with my mom and dad in Twin Valley as my sons, who were early risers, played out back in the fenced in yard, Teresa and Bobby were standing outside my front door in Cleveland.

Bobby lifted little Cindy, his three-year-old daughter, through an open window off my front porch. It was a window that wouldn't lock despite all of my efforts to the contrary. Bobby had made sure my repair efforts had been failures so he could get inside my house when I was gone to work.

The first time he had tried this little stunt was when Eddy, my oldest boy, wanted his favorite toy that was inside my locked house. Bobby scouted the house a bit and discovered a window that would pull down from the top. He picked up Eddy and lifted him in through the window.

"Eddy, go open the front door so I can help you find your toy," whispered Bobby.

Eddy ran to the front door and turned the lock to allow Bobby to enter the house. Bobby claimed to be looking for Eddy's toy but he was actually checking out the place to see if there was anything worth stealing and selling.

Eddy found his toy and went searching for Bobby. He saw Bobby in my bedroom looking inside my closet.

"Mommy doesn't let anyone in her closet," said Eddy as he quietly walked into the room.

"I thought I heard something. Maybe a mouse or rat? You wouldn't want something like that to jump out and scare your mommy would you?"

"No," whispered a frightened Eddy as he backed away from the closet and out of the room.

"I guess I must be hearing things," said Bobby as he pushed some clothes aside to see the floor of the closet. "There's nothing here now. Don't tell your mommy about this. It might scare her. Okay?"

Eddy nodded in agreement.

After Bobby closed the front window that Eddy had used to get inside the house, he and Eddy walked out the front door locking it behind them.

That little exercise of getting into my house was almost a daily occurrence that was a wonderful secret that Eddy kept from me with Bobby's encouragement until I started searching for the truth.

Bobby had taught Cindy, his own daughter, how to do the same thing so that he could get into my house any time he wanted or needed to do so.

"Open the front door, Cindy. Hurry up now. Let daddy in," commanded Bobby as Teresa looked on.

Cindy enjoyed playing the game of climbing through the window and opening the front door. She knew her daddy would be so proud of her.

As soon as the front door was unlocked, Bobby and Teresa entered the house so they could pack up my belongings as well as their own. They didn't want all of my things. They were going to pick and choose and take what they could use or sell to make a little spending money.

"We'll have to ransack the place to make it look like someone broke in and robbed Ellen. We don't want it to look like we did it," said Bobby as he hastily turned over the living room sofa scattering the cushions. After they removed everything usable from the living room, they turned over tables breaking the figurines and glassware, scattered magazines, bills, and several pieces of paper.

Just because he wanted to be evil, Bobby took one sofa cushion and placed it with the items they were taking.

"Why do you want that?" asked a confused Teresa.

"Need it for packing some of our stuff in the truck," he explained as he proceeded to the kitchen to do some more destruction.

He didn't need the cushion. He knew that if he took it with him I would have to buy another sofa.

The kitchen contained only one item that interested Bobby. He wanted the small freezer filled with frozen food. He had seen me carrying the groceries into the house so he knew it was full.

"We'll get this last. We don't want it to thaw and ruin the food when we drive to my mom and dad's house," said Bobby as he pointed to the freezer.

"Do you want anything else in here?" asked Teresa,

"Grab the small appliances. We could use those or sell them, whatever. Get the phone, too. After you pull everything from the cabinets onto the floor, then we can go upstairs."

"Tell me again why we're tearing up this place, Bobby?" asked Teresa as she pulled a bag of flour to the floor spreading the white powder everywhere.

"We want the cops to think it was ransacked by the thieves."

"We're the thieves and that's what we're doing."

"Yeah, but Ellen would never believe we did this; especially not you, Teresa. You are her only friend that I know of. Have you ever seen or heard Ellen talk to or about any other women friends?"

"No, not one."

"Let's go upstairs."

They grabbed everything they saw in my sons' bedroom. They took all the toys, clothes, and even the furniture.

"Our kids can use all of this," said Bobby as he and Teresa carried all of the items downstairs.

"We've still got to go through Ellen's bedroom," said Teresa. "There are some things in there that I want.

We wear about the same size clothes so I want most of those. And, I want her jewelry box. It's full of pretty things that she never wears. Such shiny, pretty things…" she added dreamily.

"Well, hurry up so we can get out of here," Bobby harshly whispered.

Teresa emptied the clothes closet of items she wanted. She rambled through the drawers of the dresser and chest taking one of the drawers to use in lieu of a box. She grabbed the jewelry box shoving it into the drawer she was taking with her.

"This will teach her not to give me my money," mumbled Teresa as she laughed evilly.

That night after the sun dropped from the sky, Bobby and Teresa, with the help of a couple of male cousins from Bobby's side of the family, loaded up a large rented truck with their household furnishings along with most of mine.

They were gone from Cleveland long before daylight Sunday morning. They were on their way a couple of hundred miles southwest of Cleveland to the city of Pomeroy to temporarily live with Bobby's parents. At least, they would stay there until things cooled down in Cleveland.

"Ellen will think a stranger robbed her house after we left. That's what she gets for not paying you Teresa. You said she still owes you about three hundred dollars. This little trick should pay what she owes you and then some. I won't have anyone cheating you, Teresa."

I owed Teresa twenty-five dollars that I was planning to pay her in a couple of days. I didn't owe her three hundred dollars like she told Bobby. On the contrary, Teresa had that baby-sitting money I paid her hidden away so Bobby couldn't get at it. She had to lie and say that I hadn't paid her for some of the baby-sitting she had done so she could keep the money. She didn't want Bobby drinking it up.

The long drive back to Cleveland was lonely for me because I left my boys with their grandparents for a two-week visit.

The sights, sounds, and smells I had enjoyed in the company of my children had faded away to stale, dull odors that induced sadness and loneliness.

I thought I would enjoy the two-week break from the bustling, topsy-turvy world of raising two sons as a single mother.

For two whole weeks I wouldn't have to worry about getting them ready to go stay with the baby-sitter. I might even be able to go out on a date if I got asked and not have to worry about getting home late or maybe even stay out all night. I would have two weeks of freedom from breaking up the brotherly squabbles, washing their dirty, dingy clothes, and washing their squirming bodies as they ducked and dived away from the washcloth.

I could list many reasons why I should be happy with my two weeks of freedom, but right then, right at that moment, I wanted to stop the car, turn it around, and go back to get my babies. I missed them so much it hurt.

I turned on the car radio searching for a distraction. As I drove closer and closer to my home in Cleveland, a dark cloud of despair seemed to color my thoughts.

The sun was shining brightly when I pulled into my driveway past my baby-sitter's house up to my parking place in front of my own rented house.

As I put the gear into park, I glanced up to see my front door standing open.

I lingered for a few moments in the car as I tried to decide whether or not I should go inside the house alone.

"They've had all weekend. I'm sure they're gone by now. God, please let them be gone," I prayed.

I exited my car slowly, leaving the door standing open. I didn't want to startle anyone with the banging car door.

I ducked down and walked to my front door as if I were hiding behind a hedge of greenery for protection.

I knew I must have looked really strange to any observer as I sneaked up on my own house.

I strained my ears for any foreign out of place sounds. I searched the area in front of me with my eyes darting from place to place looking for signs of disturbance.

I arrived at my front door and poked my head around it as I kept my body shielded behind the door away from the sight of anyone inside.

I heard nothing, no sounds of anyone plundering.

My eyes caught a hint of the destruction as I glanced at the stairway in the front entrance hall that led to the second floor. Small broken toys and soiled clothing were scattered down the steps pointing the path to despair and depression.

I called the police, but the officers who finally showed up two hours later didn't seem to want to be bothered by my trivial problem.

They sloughed if off as another domestic dispute but promised they would look into the disappearance of Bobby, Teresa, and family.

Then they left to file their report and I never heard from them again about the investigation into the theft of my personal articles and the theft of my sons' toys and clothing.

That's the day I resolved to locate my own belongings through yard sales.

I had started over so many times in the past. I didn't think I had the strength or the desire to do it again.

I asked my mom and dad to take care of my boys as I searched for my past every Saturday. Depression consumed me during every waking moment. All I was able to do was focus on what was taken from me. I had to find them, the necklace and the ring. I had to restore my life to what it was before the theft. Finding the necklace and the ring was the only way my mind would deal with it. Then – only then – could I go on living my life.

Months had passed and it became too late for the law to do anything to Teresa and Bobby for destroying my life, but that didn't matter to me anymore. I wasn't really interested in making them pay. I had surpassed the desire for revenge and punishment.

All I wanted to do was to find the necklace my grandmother had given me and retrieve my high school ring.

The fact that the items had been loaded up and taken over two hundred miles away from the area I intended to search never entered my tortured mind.

The weather was turning colder so I knew that there would not be many more yard sales left to search this season.

I had walked a great deal further than normal, but I knew my time was running out which would eliminate my chance to free my mind from this all-consuming obsession.

The street I was following was an alley of sorts that I had never seen or walked on before in all of my many yard sale searches.

It was a dark, dingy alley even in the daytime. The buildings and trees seemed to shroud the alley from prying eyes.

I was so tired from searching all day. I thought that maybe my tiredness made my mood dark causing the alley to appear uninviting.

There seemed to be only a couple of houses or apartments facing the alley and one of them had yard sale items scattered about for bargain hunters to see.

I wondered how many customers they have had. *Not many would even dare to walk down this alley*, I thought as I continued to walk past the garbage cans and dilapidated garages to the yard sale area.

The only ray of sunshine evident in the alley was shining directly onto the yard sale items. While everything in and around the alley appeared dull, dirty, and dilapidated, the yard sale items were glistening and spotlessly clean.

Maybe it's just my tired eyes, I thought as I started touching the glistening items to see if they were real.

My eyes fell on a ring, a high school ring. It looked so much like my ring that I was afraid to touch it. I didn't want to be disappointed.

I turned the ring over in my hands. It looked just like my own ring, but then hundreds of rings would look just like mine. After all, it was a high school ring.

I moved the ring closer to my eyes so I could see if it was engraved. It had the correct year, but if it was mine, it would be engraved with an "EH" inside the band.

The "EH" seemed to dance against the gold of the ring band.

"Where did you get this ring?" I asked as I smiled.

No one answered. No one was there. No one was watching me as I looked at the items for sale.

I clutched the ring in my hand and continued to look at the other items.

I looked at sheets and blankets that all seemed familiar, but I knew they could have very easily belonged to someone else. I certainly didn't corner the market on the design and quality of the dollar store linens.

Still, no one was around to take my money, to answer my questions.

Suddenly I saw the age worn jewelry box.

"It's my jewelry box!" I shouted as I reached for it to snatch it from the rickety table on which it was displayed.

Inside the box was the old gold tone necklace I had bought when I received my first paycheck. There were many trinkets that I had received from family members and friends.

I moved the trinkets aside and opened the hidden compartment inside the jewelry box where I saw the pearl necklace I had been looking for each and every Saturday.

Tears were streaming down my face as I clutched the jewelry box to my breast and close to my heart.

Still no one was around. No one was there to answer my questions or take my money.

I sat on a chair next to the table. I would wait for a while. Maybe they would be back soon.

I slipped the ring on to my finger and held the jewelry box in my lap.

I was so tired.

I must have fallen asleep because when I opened my eyes, it was dark. Everything was gone with only the jewelry box remaining on my lap and the ring on my finger.

There were no electric lights to be seen; only the moonlight illuminated my path through the alley as I walked home.

I'll go back tomorrow, I thought as I looked around me to see if I were being followed.

The sinister darkness made the hairs on the back of my neck rise. Chills rolled down my spine causing me to shudder. I was frightened, truly frightened.

That night my dreams were happy and centered on my sons and parents.

The next morning I rose early to pack up what belongings I had so I could travel south and return to my family and life again.

First, I had to have some answers about my ring and jewelry box.

I walked to where I had found the alley the previous day.

"It was here," I whispered as I looked around for a familiar sight. "I know I was here - it was here."

No alley, nothing looked vaguely familiar.

I was there. I walked down that alley, I thought in total confusion.

I saw an elderly man walking along the street.

"Do you live around here, Mister?" I asked excitedly.

"All my life," he politely replied.

"Is there an alley around here? I saw it yesterday, but I seemed to have lost my bearings. Can you point me to the right direction?" I pleaded.

"No, no alley, Ma'am. Never been an alley anywhere near here that I have ever seen. You aren't the first to ask about that alley. Seems to me there was a lady about this time last year that stopped me to ask me the same question," he said as he scratched his chin.

"Are you sure there's no alley?"

"No alley, nowhere around here. Why are you looking for it?"

"I wanted to pay for the items I picked up at the yard sale."

"That's what that other lady said. Said she found some things that had been stolen from her. Is that what happened to you?" he questioned curiously.

"Yes, it is," I answered meekly.

"I'd say it was just His way of returning back to you what was taken. What do you think?" he said as he smiled revealing the toothless gums of a denture wearer without his dentures.

"I don't know what to think," I said as I responded to the smile with one of my own. "I'm leaving town and I want to pay for the things I took home with me,"

"Don't worry about it, Lady. He will know your new address, won't He?"

"I guess," I said as I glanced down at my feet.

When I looked up to thank him for his help, he was gone.

I left the city that day to join my waiting family and begin to live again.

CHAPTER 13
IN YOUR BEST INTEREST

Not all surprises are bad…

The waitress appeared in front of us and handed me a note. I unfolded it and glanced at the words.

> "It's in your best interest to meet me at 7 P.M. tonight, alone, at Pine and Stillwell Avenue."

There was no signature.

"Who is it from?" asked Sandy as her curiosity was bubbling over.

"It isn't signed."

"Let me see it. Maybe I can recognize the handwriting."

"It's typed. But here, take a look," I said as I handed the note to Sandy.

Sandy stared at the note. She didn't like the vibrations that were emanating from the folded paper. Secrets, too many secrets were hidden on that small piece of paper.

The day was beautiful. The sun was shining brightly and the temperature was near seventy degrees.

The small restaurant was busy with people milling around looking for vacant seats, meeting and greeting their friends.

"Who do you think it's from?" asked Sandy as she refolded the note carefully handing it back to me as if it were burning her fingers.

"I don't have any idea. There's nobody here that would have a reason to give me a note like this. I just don't know what to think about this. Why are you acting like you are afraid to hold that piece of paper?" I asked as I glanced around the crowded room.

"Just a feeling like there is a really, deep, dark secret surrounding that note buried in those words."

"Maybe it's just a joke," said Sandy letting doubt creep into her voice.

"Not funny, is it?"

"No, it's not. Take it back to work. Maybe you can show it around there and see if anyone recognizes the handwrit---- oh, never mind. I forgot. It's typed. Is it printed by computer? Or typewriter? Let me look at it again," said Sandy with sudden inspiration.

"It looks to me like it's not a typewriter. It's done on a computer and printed on laser jet," I said I handed the note back to Sandy.

"Yeah, that's a common, ordinary laser jet. We won't be able to trace that, will we?"

"No, they are all just alike print-wise."

"What do you think it's about?" questioned Sandy.

"I don't know. I haven't done anything to anybody that I know of."

"What are you going to do?"

"I don't know that either."

"You're not going to meet this person, are you?"

"Maybe. How else can I discover what this is all about?"

"Ellen, please don't. It could be some kind of killer or rapist."

"I know, I know. I'll ask the waitress to tell us who gave her the note."

The place was busy and it was hard trying to attract the attention of the waitress who knew she didn't have to attend to our table anymore except to clean it up after we paid and left.

"Jerri," I whispered loudly towards the waitress.

She glanced at me and nodded her head.

I waited nervously for her to finish taking the orders from the table she was attending to across the room from me.

"Jerri, this note you handed to me, do you remember who gave it to you?"

"No, some guy I never saw before said to give it to the lady with blonde hair and blue dress. That has to be you," she said as she pointed to my bright blue dress and then my dark blonde hair.

"Do you remember what he looked like?"

"Hey, I've got to get back to work. I really don't remember the guy. I was busy then like I'm busy now," she said as she hurried away towards the kitchen to place her orders for the table across the room.

"How would the guy know what I was wearing today unless he had been watching me? Am I being stalked? My husband surely wouldn't tell a complete stranger what I was wearing, would he?" I asked myself verbally so that Sandy could hear my thoughts.

Sandy shrugged her shoulders and looked around the crowded room trying to find the unwanted glance at me from a stranger lurking about with guilt plastered across his face.

Sandy and I tried to finish eating our salads so we could walk back to work on this beautiful, sunny day.

I had no idea what I was going to do. I racked my brain trying to figure out who in the world could have sent me such an intriguing note, maybe I should describe it as scary because intriguing doesn't seem to be strong enough to convey to anyone the feelings I was having.

I looked at people who were working around me trying to determine if one of them could have had the note delivered. No, no, I don't think so. I'm sure the waitress would know most of people I work with because living in a small town, there just weren't that many eating establishments. If you were a stranger, you didn't remain a stranger for very long because everyone would know you or know of you before much time passed.

If not people I work with, who could it be? My life was limited in the number of people I would meet and greet every day. I worked and I went home. I did very little else because of monetary constraints. There was absolutely no one in my life that would want to meet me at Pine and Stillwell Avenue at seven.

Maybe it was a family member. I hadn't seen my brother in many years, but there was no reason he couldn't come walking up to my front door to say hello. Miles are what kept us apart. An occasional telephone call and a Christmas card were usually the only contacts I had with him during the year.

Cousins? I had some but I really didn't know who they were except my two female first cousins on my mother's side. All my other cousins were complete and total strangers to me.

Uncles? I had a couple of them. Uncle Jim was the strange one. He was a loner, a recluse who didn't stray too far from home. His home was forty miles south of where I live so I really didn't expect to see him on a street corner. Besides, he was getting up there in years and we never were too friendly with each other back when I was a kid or now.

Aunts? No, it was a man that gave the waitress the note.

It certainly wasn't my husband and it surely would not be either of my two sons. One son, Eddy, lived a few miles up the road from me but Aaron, my second son, lived in Nebraska.

Who could it be?

My work was getting in the way of my thinking and day dreaming about the clandestine meeting that I knew I would attend. At five o'clock, thankfully, I prepared myself of go home and start what I called the second shift of washing clothes, making dinner, etc., etc., etc.

I didn't tell my husband that I was meeting someone at seven. I didn't want him to worry, or try to talk me out of it, or go with me. I wanted to handle this problem all by myself so that if I got into some kind a trouble, it would only be me, trying to get out of that same trouble. My husband would call me stupid for going alone, Sandy would call me brave, while all I could call myself was stubborn.

"Sonny, I'm going to run to the Dollar Store and grab some things for work. I'll be right back."

"Do you want me to go with you," he asked knowing that I would say no.

"No, you watch your ballgame. I'll be right back," I said as I let the door slam behind me.

My daddy always told me that there were two major things I inherited from him. The first thing was not so proper for a lady, but it was so true; I inherited the ability to sweat like a race horse. Perspiration would pour off me when I was working outside in the sun just like it did off of him all summer long when he worked in his garden. The second thing, the trait I couldn't deny, was his stubbornness that filled every crack and crevice of my mind and body. He always told me my stubbornness would get me into big trouble someday. I was wondering if that someday had arrived.

I circled the block several times as I looked for a man waiting at Pine and Stillwell Avenue. I saw a jogger and a couple of teens walking along Stillwell Avenue but no one else. Maybe I needed to park the car and get out so whoever it was would know I was there waiting. Then again, maybe not.

After a couple of more trips around the block, I knew I had to do something.

I pulled over to the side of the road in front of a house that had stood vacant for many months. When I looked at it, I realized someone had moved into it because there were draperies at the windows through which inside lighting could be see filtering through the threads of the fabric.

I stood in front of the house at Pine and Stillwell Avenue staring at the newly adorned windows, not paying any attention to my surroundings when I felt a tap on my shoulder. I whirled around and came face to face with my son Aaron, who was supposed to be Nebraska.

"Surprise, Mom," he said as he threw his arms around me. "I'm home. I'm here to stay. Welcome to my house."

He led me by the arm into the house on Pine and Stillwell Avenue. When I glanced behind me, I saw my husband and son, Eddy, following me.

CHAPTER 14
WRONG NUMBER

Some of my bad confrontations had been pure, out and out, accidents that should never have happened…

"Hi, Molly, what you got for sale today?" I asked as I walked through Molly's front yard to get to the items strewn around on her porch under a sign indicating "garage sale" in bold red letters large enough for the world to see from the street.

"It's just some stuff I picked up at an auction the other day. There's a lot more in the garage. I put some of it out front here to get everybody's attention."

I walked slowly through the strewn articles that were showy and attention grabbing. My interests were drawn to more useful objects even though I liked to look at the pretty, shiny objects just as much as the next person.

I needed some bed linens, towels, and curtains if I could find any at a reasonable price. As a single mother of two growing boys, I found it difficult trying to keep up with even the bare necessities of life.

"Molly, have you got any useful stuff?"

"Check the garage. There are even some toys and games in there."

I wandered on to the garage and started searching through the boxes and tables that were set out for view.

I liked to rummage through yard and garage sales. More times than not, I tended to spend more than I should, but everything I bought was at a rock bottom price. I wouldn't have been able to purchase most of the frivolous items that filled our world without infiltrating the world of "second hand", "used", or "previously owned."

As I told my sons, "No one needs to know we didn't buy them new."

Sometimes I would get cheated. That's happened a couple of times when I purchased a small appliance from someone who swore to God and Heaven above that the item was as good as new. When I arrived home and plugged it into the electricity, it was a wonder that I hadn't started a house fire from all the sparking and sputtering that occurred in the wall socket. But, those are the chances you have to take when you are shopping among people you don't know. They may live in your small town, but that doesn't mean that they are honest. I didn't bother to return the item. I just chalked it up to stupidity and swore that the next time I would make them plug it into an outlet while I was standing and watching, before I paid my hard earned money for the junk.

I purchased a four slice toaster that would only toast two slices at a time. It would do until I could get something better.

I couldn't find any decent bed linens. The curtains were faded, dark colors that I wouldn't want for any reason. There were no towels in the garage at all. Not a good day to shop for what I needed so I started looking in other areas.

The boys wanted some board games so they could invite some friends over for the night and try their level best to make me crazy. I guess that's one of the prices you pay for being a mother.

"Hey, Molly, have you got any board games?" I yelled from the garage to the front yard.

"I think so, Ellen. Look in the box in the back in the corner to the right."

It was fun exploring through the boxes of things I didn't need. It was like Christmas shopping at a rate I could afford.

Everything was dusty and grimy in the boxes in the back of the garage. I guess that's why Molly set them back there. She hadn't had enough time to go through them and sort out the good from the bad. I supposed that might be good because she hadn't had time to set a really good price meaning perhaps I could buy them a little cheaper than the already cheap price I knew she would give them.

I found a Clue Game that looked like it was short a couple of pieces. Scrabble suffered from the same problem. The Monopoly Game looked almost new. The cellophane wrapping was partially attached. It looked as if someone had opened the game box and peeked inside without removing any of the game pieces.

I picked up the game and walked to the front of the house where Molly was taking care of a couple of buying visitors. I stood to the side and waited.

"Molly," I said after the purchasers cleared out, "how much for the game?"

"Did you get it out of the box in the back?"

"Yes."

"I haven't gone through those boxes with a fine tooth comb yet. You might be able to find some real treasures in there that I don't even know about," she said with a smile.

"I'm just interested in the game, if it doesn't cost too much."

"You have two boys, don't you?"

"Yes, why?"

"No reason. Does a dollar sound good?"

"Sounds great to me."

"I hope you and your boys have fun playing the game."

"We will," I said with a big smile. "They are going to be so surprised."

As soon as I arrived home, I gathered up my sons who had been playing with the neighborhood kids around my mom's house, and took them inside where we could explore the new game. My mom lived a couple of houses away from mine so babysitting was no problem for me. The fact that I could trust my mom with my boys and not worry about them being mistreated in any way, made having to work for a living a little bit easier.

"Eddy, pull the rest of the cellophane off the box so we can play the game," I told my eldest as I pushed the box to him from my side of the table.

"Let me do it," shouted Aaron as he reached for the box.

"I told Eddy to do it, Aaron. You can do it the next time," I said as I tried to calm the minor eruption of temper from my youngest son.

"He gets to do everything," Aaron remarked sullenly as he crossed his arms in front of his chest and plastered a pout on his young face.

Eddy pulled the cellophane lose and jumped down from his chair to throw it into the trash can.

Aaron saw the opportunity to reach across the table and grab the box. He removed the lid and pulled out the game board. He placed it in the center of the table and searched around in the box for the play pieces.

"I want the shoe," shouted Eddy as he watched his little brother searched though the pieces.

"Give those to me, Aaron," I said as I held out my hand. I bunched the pieces up in my hand, shook them around, and then had the boys draw out the piece they would play with. It was the easiest way to prevent a knock down drag out fight.

"Get the cards out, Aaron. We need the two sets of cards before we start playing."

Aaron had never played Monopoly before so I knew I was going to have to help him until he could get the hang of it.

As Aaron placed the cards on the game board, a small piece of paper fell from the stack.

I reached for the piece of paper. I knew it didn't belong with the game.

There was a phone number printed by a shaky hand on the paper in pencil along with the words "please call." I folded the paper and shoved it in my pants pocket. I would take care of it later after my boys went to bed when I could have a little privacy.

Eddy had played the game previously so he knew how to beat the pants off of Aaron and me. Aaron didn't like losing but I knew he would get over it and would most likely win the next time. Aaron was a quick learner and it only takes one loss to make him a better player.

As soon as I forced the boys into bed, I pulled the paper from my pocket and reread it. I wasn't sure if I should dial that telephone number or not but my curiosity got the best of me.

It was ringing – one – two – three – four – five times and no one was answering. I was about to place the receiver back into its cradle when I heard a weak "Hello."

I jerked the phone back and placed the receiver against my head, "Hello" I shouted in the mouthpiece. I knew I sounded angry. I wasn't angry, just surprised.

"May I help you?" asked the weak voice.

What was I going to say? What was I going to tell her was my reason for calling?

"My name is Ellen, Ellen Hutchins. I know this is going to sound really strange, but I found a piece of paper with your telephone number on it and the words "please call." I found the paper in a game of Monopoly that I bought for my two sons. Are you the one who put the paper in the Monopoly box?"

There was silence on the other end.

"Hello, are you still there?" I whispered into the telephone.

"Yes, yes, I'm here."

"Did you put that paper in the Monopoly box?" I questioned in a soft tone.

"Yes."

"Are you all right? Do you need help?"

"No, I'm fine," explained the weak voice.

"Why did you put that note in the Monopoly box?"

"I'm sorry, but I can't tell you over the telephone. Do you think you could stop by my house someday and I'll tell you the reason?"

"Why?"

"You said you wanted to know?" she sputtered.

"No, I mean why do I have to come to your house? Why don't you tell me over the phone?"

"I just can't. My name is Nellie Long. My address is Grove Village Estates; it's a mobile home park in Duran. Do you know where that is?"

"Yes."

"When will you stop by?"

"Would tomorrow be all right with you?"

"What time tomorrow?"

"It would have to be after work. Would five o'clock be good?"

"Yes, it would. You have children? You said you bought the game for your two sons? You can bring them with you. They will be more than welcome," she said with happiness dripping from her voice.

We said our good-byes and I hung up the telephone wondering about what I had gotten myself into with this silly phone call.

It was hard to focus on my tasks at work. I kept wondering about my appointment with an old lady I had never met. What was she going to tell me about the reason for the telephone number in the Monopoly box? Was she being mistreated by family members? Was she being held captive by mean and cruel relatives? Was she planning to harm me and my boys? Should I take my sons with me? She seemed so happy to think that my boys were also going to visit her. What should I do?

An entire day of wondering and worrying did not help me find a solution. I drove home after work, picked up Eddy and Aaron, and drove to Duran which was about twenty miles away from my house. I knew the area and the trailer park because, when we first moved to Virginia, that was where we lived, in that very same trailer park.

"Where are we going, Mom?" asked Eddy as he was trying to figure out what was going on and why he had to leave his favorite television show.

"We are going to visit someone," I said as a vague explanation.

"Who?"

"Her name is Nellie Long."

"Why?"

"She wants to meet us."

"Why?"

"I really don't know, Eddy. I found her phone number written on a piece of paper in your Monopoly game box. I called it and she invited us to her house. That's all I know. Don't keep asking me questions, okay?"

Eddy could tell I was irritated. He wasn't sure if I was mad at him or someone else. He didn't ask any more questions.

Aaron wasn't so curious. He liked to visit other people. He was a people watcher and an explorer so he didn't mind the sudden, unplanned trip to Duran. It was a change of scenery, something new for his mind and eyes to digest.

I was going into this with apprehension laced with fear. I rationalized the whole situation by saying "it's just a little old lady" to myself over and over again. Something was bothering me, but I didn't know what it was.

I just wasn't ready to stop the car and enter into something I wasn't sure of as I dragged my two sons with me. I drove around the trailer park a couple of times. I knew exactly where the trailer was located because I had lived in that trailer park before moving to Stillwell.

"Come on, Boys, let's get out of the car and go knock on the door," I said as I eyed the closed front door of the old, but well maintained, mobile home. All of the dark curtains were closed to prevent any infiltration of sunlight. *That's odd*, I thought, she must be sensitive to sunlight.

I stood on the wooden stoop in front of the door with my sons standing in front of me and I knocked on the door softly. No one answered so I knocked harder. *She must be hard of hearing,* I mused.

The door swung open but no little old lady appeared.

"Come in, come in," said a weak sounding voice from behind the door in the total darkness. The light from the setting, evening sun was bouncing off of the mobile home and had blinded all three of us as we proceeded to walk slowly into the home.

My eyes finally started adjusting to the darkness and I prodded my sons to step forward.

"Please sit down," said the bodiless voice from the darkest corner of the room

I pushed the boys ahead of me to the sofa where I sat down with Eddy at my right and Aaron at my left. It was always better to keep them separated.

"Mrs. Long, this is Eddy," I said as I lifted my right arm slightly pointing it at my eldest son. "This young man right here is Aaron," I continued with a flourish of my left arm.

Suddenly the front door closed with a bang that rattled the walls.

I jumped up from the sofa.

My boys screamed.

I knew it was a mistake coming here.

"Mrs. Long, what is going on?" I screamed at the darkness.

"Sit down, Ellen; you and your sons need to sit down now!"

The voice that issued that command was no longer that of a weak, elderly lady.

"What do you want?" I said in a tone that was defiant and scared.

"Money."

"You've got to be kidding," I said sarcastically. "I don't have any money. I'm a divorced mother of two kids who is just barely getting by. Where would I get money?"

"I'm sure you could find some if push came to shove," growled the voice from the darkness.

"Where? How?"

"You've got friends and family, don't you?"

"A few friends and even fewer relatives."

There was silence in the room. My young sons were wordless I would guess due to the fear emanating from me.

"Are you still there?" I asked the darkness.

No answer - silence was reigning supreme.

I ran to the door and twisted the knob. It was locked. I knew it would be. No surprise there. I felt around the knob searching for a lock that I could push or turn. I hadn't heard anyone lock the door from the outside and, because of the almost total darkness inside, I hadn't seen anyone lock it from this side of the door.

"Mommy, Mommy," whimpered Aaron as he tried to find me.

"Right here, Baby. Don't worry. I'm right here," I said as I reached out for his blonde head to pull him towards me.

With Aaron came the frightened Eddy and they both hugged my legs searching for comfort and protection from what – we didn't have a clue.

"Is anyone here?" I demanded as the boys and I started walking through the trailer searching for a way out.

"Mommy, I want to go home," pleaded Aaron as he held onto my hand as if it were the only thing allowing him to walk on this Earth.

"Soon, Baby, soon. You and Eddy stay really close to me all the time. You have to walk with me every time I walk. I don't want you guys going anywhere where I can't touch you. Do you understand?"

I was sure they were nodding their heads up and down in affirmation, but I wanted a verbal answer.

"Do you understand me?" I asked harshly.

"Yes, yes," were the timid echoed answers.

I walked from room to room dragging my frightened sons with me as I searched for a way out of this mess.

Why did I call that number? They must think I'm someone else. They think I actually have money to pay them or a source with deep pockets that could give them the money for the release of me and my boys. They've got to have me mixed up with someone else.

Maybe that phone number wasn't meant for me. Maybe I got it by accident. Who in the world would they think would get the message? If I get out of this mess, when I get out of this mess, I'm going to talk to Molly. She could tell me where she bought the box that contained the Monopoly Game.

"Ellen," said the disembodied voice from the darkness.

"What is it you want from me?"

"Nothing, I'm afraid we have made a mistake."

"You sure have."

"You will find the front door unlocked. You must not reveal to anyone what has happened here this evening. There will be a deadly price to pay if you talk of this to anyone at any time."

"I won't say a word," I babbled as I herded my sons toward the front door and the freedom that lay in wait on the other side. I was afraid that I was going to get a bullet in my back before I was able to run to freedom pushing my boys in front of me to hurry them along.

I reached for the doorknob and turned it slowly. I was surprised when I felt the turning in my hand.

"Come on, Guys, run to the car as fast as you can."

They took off running at lightning speed with me bringing up the rear. Into the car we jumped and I started the engine before I got the door completely closed.

"Fasten your seatbelts while we get out of here," I told my sons who usually had to fasten those seatbelts before I would put the car into gear.

I glanced back and saw no lights – nothing – the mobile home remained dark.

I fed my boys and put them to bed. Before the night was over, both of my young sons had crawled into my bed. I didn't scold them. I knew they had been scared just as much as I had been. It would take a while to get this act of random kindness on my part to be pushed back to the back burner. All I wanted to do was help a little old lady. I didn't think I was wrong.

"Come on, Boys, you've got to go to grandma's house so I can go to work. Hurry up, will you?"

That's the usual start for each and every day. I had hopes that the rest of the day would be "usual." The phone call dashed my hopes beyond recognition.

"Mrs. Hutchins, this is Eddy's teacher. My name is Sarah Carson."

"Is Eddy okay?" I asked as I started to panic.

"Eddy is fine, Mrs. Hutchins. Well, not quite fine. He seemed jumpy and upset today so I asked him if he had a problem he wanted to talk about."

"What's the problem? I didn't know he had a problem."

"Eddy says that he was scared that you would take him back to the trailer where he was locked up. Do you know what he is talking about?"

"Yes, Ma'am, it was a misunderstanding. And no – I didn't lock Eddy up anywhere."

"Eddy is very upset. When I tried to question him some more, he burst into tears. Is there a problem, Mrs. Hutchins?"

"I'll leave work right now and pick up both Eddy and Aaron."

"How long will it be before you arrive at the school?"

"About a half hour."

"I will get Aaron from his classroom and have both boys waiting for you in principal's office."

They think I'm abusing my boys.

I drove to the school like a robot.

I entered the school without a smile on my face and signed my two sons out of school with the minimum amount of words exchanged with the clerks and principal. The very idea that I was abusing my sons was beyond my comprehension. I loved my boys more than life itself. I would never intentionally endanger the lives of my babies in any way.

All I had wanted to do when I went to meet the little old lady was adopt a grandmother for my sons.

"Eddy, your teacher thinks I locked you up somewhere to punish you. Did you tell her that?" I probed softly because I knew Eddy would become sullen and unresponsive.

"No, that's not what I said."

"What did you say?"

"I said we were all locked up in that trailer. It wasn't just me," he looked at me with pleading eyes.

"Why did you tell her anything at all?"

"I don't know. She asked me if there was something wrong and that's when I told her."

"Were you sad or crying?"

"No, I wasn't paying attention. She called on me and I didn't know the answer. She said she would get back to me during recess. I didn't want to miss recess. So that's what I told her."

"I don't want you telling anyone else about the trailer. Okay? That man told us not to tell anyone. Don't you remember that?"

Eddy shook his head in agreement.

"Can I watch television, Mom?" he asked as I heard a knock at the door.

"Sure, go ahead. Watch something you both want to see."

I ran to the front door where I saw a stranger, a woman, standing in front of me holding out some kind of badge.

"Are you Mrs. Hutchins?" she demanded.

"I'm Ellen Hutchins. Who are you?" I demanded equally as harsh.

"I'm Amy Varner with the Department of Social Services. I'm here to investigate a child abuse charge."

"Oh, my God," I cried as I forced myself not to slam the door in her face.

"Mrs. Hutchins, may I come in?"

I opened the door wider and pointed toward the living room sofa.

"What is this about?" I asked when I regained control of my emotions.

"An anonymous caller stated that you locked your sons up in a dark trailer. Is that true?" she asked with eyes that were displaying doubt from the onset of the questions.

"The truth is, me along with my sons were locked up in that trailer. So – I guess the answer would have to be yes but I wasn't doing the locking," I said sarcastically.

How could such an innocent act of kindness get so blown out of proportion?

"I don't understand. Start from the beginning, Mrs. Hutchins."

"The man who was holding us for what he thought would be ransom told us not to tell anyone about what had happened. I believed him when he said we would pay a deadly price if we did talk."

"Mrs. Hutchins, are you trying to say that your life was threatened?"

"Yes, Ma'am, I am. The man who locked us up said he wanted money. All I was trying to do was befriend a lonely old lady. When I told him I didn't have any money, he suddenly changed his mind. I truly think he lured in the wrong family. He thought we were another family who had money, obviously."

"Did you know this man? Have you contacted the police?"

"No, I didn't know him. Would you have contacted the police?"

"I most certainly would."

"Ms. Varner, do you have children?"

There was a pause.

"No, but I would want to do the right thing," she sputtered as she looked for a reason.

"My sons are my reason for not calling the police. I don't want them growing up without a mother who loves them very much. In the alternative, I don't want to have to face the world each day knowing that I caused the death of one or both of my sons. What do you think? Did I do the right thing?"

"Mrs. Hutchins, may I speak with your sons?"

"Sure, no problem," I answered in an agreeable tone even though the last thing I wanted to be was agreeable. Actually I wanted to reach out and grab hold of that teacher's neck for interfering and maybe causing the deaths of my sons and me.

I walked out of the room to get Eddy who had secreted himself away in his bedroom.

"Eddy, Ms. Varner wants to talk to you," I said as I introduced him to Amy Varner, Social Worker.

"Eddy, I need to ask you about the trailer. Who locked you in that trailer?"

"I don't know. It was dark. We never got to see his face," he answered as he looked down at the floor.

"Who was with you?"

"My mommy and brother were locked up with me. We couldn't get out. Mommy walked us from room to room looking for another door, but we couldn't find one."

"Do you know why he did that to you? Lock you up, I mean?"

"No, mommy said we were going to visit a little old lady who needed a friend. That's all we were doing."

"Could you tell me where the trailer was?"

"It was in Duran, in the trailer park where we used to live."

"And you didn't know the person who did this to you?"

"No."

"Do you remember seeing a number on the trailer?"

"Yeah, it had number 13."

Amy Varner looked up at me. I shook my head in agreement.

"Thank you, Eddy. Send your brother in here. Okay?"

Aaron came running into the room and ran directly to me.

"Turn around, Aaron, Ms. Varner wants to ask you a question," I instructed my son as I tried to give him a little shove so that he would be facing Amy Varner.

"No, I don't want to."

"Do as I say, Aaron. It won't take long and it doesn't hurt, I promise."

Aaron reluctantly faced Amy Varner.

"Did someone lock you away in a trailer in Duran?"

Aaron looked at me for help.

"Just answer her question, Aaron," I said softly.

"I can't say," was his response.

"Why can't you say? Did your mommy tell you to say that?"

"No, the man did."

"Thank you, Aaron. You can go be with your brother."

"Did you get enough, Ms. Varner? Do you believe me now?" I asked angrily.

"Yes, Mrs. Hutchins. I will have to do some more investigating, but I don't believe you will have any more problems about this phone call in particular."

"Have there been other phone calls?"

"No, Ma'am, but usually when we get one phone call, we will get others."

"You won't get any about my kids. Now get out of here before I lose my temper," I said as I could feel the anger sparkling in my eyes.

"Mrs. Hutchins, I will be doing some more investigating. You will be hearing from me again," said Amy Varner as she walked through my door to the front porch.

"Good," I shouted after her. "Maybe you can tell me who the crazy man was and why he was holding us in a locked trailer."

I sort of swore off going to yard sales for a while. I didn't want a repeat of the telephone number episode to replay itself. I certainly got a wrong number that day.

I saw Molly a few days later.

"Where did you get that Monopoly Game you sold me?"

"Some guy came by here and told me I had to sell it to the lady with two little boys. You're the only one with two little boys that I knew about, at that time. Later in the day, another lady came by with two little boys in tow. She asked me for a Monopoly Game and I told her I already sold it. She said her name was Veronica Shott. She then said someone had told her about this place and that this was where she could go to get the game. She seemed real disappointed. She didn't look like she was shy on money, but something told me she was hiding out, trying to stay out of sight. Anyway, that's all I know about it. Is there a problem?"

"Do you know who the lady was?"

"Like I said, she told me she was Veronica Shott. I think she was one of <u>the</u> Shott family. They have a lot of money. I couldn't imagine why she was going to yard sales."

That had to be it. My captor thought he was getting a member of the Shott family who had amassed great fortunes during the coal mining boom.

I felt relieved. I knew I would not be lured into another locked mobile home fearing for my life as well as the lives of my two precious sons.

The phone was ringing as I was trying to unload the car of my sons and the few groceries I had picked up with what I had left over from my meager paycheck.

"Hello," I screamed into the instrument.

"Mrs. Hutchins?"

"Yes, this is Ellen Hutchins. Who are you?" I said hurriedly as I looked to see which direction my sons had run to.

"This is Amy Varner. I told you I would do some more investigating in your case. I want to report my findings to you. May I stop by your house later?" she asked politely and very business-like.

"You're not going to try to take my boys from me, are you?" I demanded. I was getting real tired of the government butting into my personal business.

"No, Ma'am. I just want to tell you what has happened."

"Fine, then you are more than welcome to visit my boys and me anytime."

Not more than a half hour later, Amy Varner was at my front door.

"Mrs. Hutchins, I would like to talk to you and your sons, if that is possible?"

"Call me Ellen. Sure, I'll go get them. They are watching television in their bedroom."

I sat my boys down beside me on the sofa. Amy Varner had positioned herself on the side chair facing the three of us.

"Ellen, you can call me Amy. I want to know if you will testify against the kidnapper who locked you up in the trailer."

"How can I do that? I never saw the man?"

"You heard his voice. You also heard his disguised voice. You heard this man as a man and as a woman. He kidnapped you and your boys. We want him locked away so he can't do this again."

"I don't think I should. What if he wants to do me and my sons harm?"

"He won't be able to. He is locked up right now. With your testimony, we don't plan to let him go."

I looked at Eddy and Aaron. "Do you think we should try to put the bad man in jail?" I asked my smiling sons.

They nodded their heads in response.

"Did you find out who he was after?" I asked Amy.

"No, but I'm sure it was someone with money."

"Well, I know who he wanted and I'm very glad his plan failed. I'm sure the woman's family would have paid lots of money for their safe return."

"Who was it?"

"What family has the most money in this whole southwest Virginia area?"

"You're not talking about the Shott family are you?"

I nodded my head in agreement.

CHAPTER 15
THOSE HABITAT PEOPLE

Why can't people be grateful when something good happens like Sonny and I were...?

Dust was everywhere but it wasn't only dust that marred the image before me. The dirt, grime, and filth that had been allowed to accumulate in a short period of time, less than a year, was unbelievable.

"Ellen, we would like for you and Sonny to do most of the cleaning of the house in Duran. It was built last year and the people that had been buying the house were made to move out and relinquish the title for nonpayment."

"Sure, we would be happy to help."

"You'll be doing most of the clean-up work alone because no one else is available. Is that a problem?"

"No, should it be?"

"You can answer that when you see the place, Ellen. You need to wear old clothes, the kind you can throw out after wearing them one more time."

"How old is this house?"

"Less than a year. I'll have someone meet you there with a key on Saturday. What time do you think you'll get there?"

"About eight in the morning. I like to get an early start."

When my mind went back to that conversation, I realized that Marlene had been trying to warn me about what I was getting into. Even if I had understood the warning, I wouldn't have believed a mother with two young children and a disabled, wheelchair bound grandfather to those children, could have caused the amount of havoc and destruction they accomplished while living in a brand new house.

As my eyes took in all the sights to be seen, I realized why no one else was available to help clean the house. Sonny and I were the newest kids on the block in this end of the county. In order to gain possession of our house, we had to clean, paint, and repair the structure after the previous owners had returned the ownership of the house to the builders, Stillwell County Habitat for Humanity.

The task Sonny and I took on in order to earn our house was minimal in comparison with what we were facing with our new assignment. In order to get our house, we had to clean baseboards, walls, shelves, and anything else that could be improved with soap and water. Then we were given gallons of paint, rollers, and brushes and were told to make the house the way we wanted it to live in it.

Our house simply required the removal of signs of the previous family which consisted of the single mother with two little girls. There was no major destruction, only the wear and tear that the family living in a home caused. My biggest worry was trying to get the color scheme in each of the rooms to fade away and die. Yellow seemed to be a favorite in every room with the exception of one wall in each room that was painted an unusually dark color such as navy blue. But, we did it. It turned out beautifully with a lot of effort on our part. Joy and happiness exuded from our pores because we were actually getting a house of our very own.

"Sonny, how could they do this? How could they treat such a wonderful opportunity as if it were an insult and punishment?" I asked as tears were streaming from my eyes.

Sonny shrugged as he looked around. He didn't have an answer for the abuse of a good thing.

A car pulled up onto the gravel driveway disgorging a couple of people who walked through the front door looking angry and upset.

"I'm Ellen and this is my husband, Sonny. Are you here to help?"

"This is supposed to be our house. Why are you here?" demanded a young woman whose age probably placed her in her early twenties.

"We came to clean. Don't you want us to help?"

I received no answer other than a glaring stare across the room.

"Sonny, let's get started," I whispered so that only he could hear. "We need to get out of here as soon as we can."

Now, keep in mind that this house is less than a year old when I tell you what we had to do to clean it up.

"Sonny, we're going to need a shovel in order to find the carpet in the living room."

"The Habitat repair trailer is out back. Maybe there is one in there."

While he was outside trying to break into the trailer because he couldn't find the key, I tried to jump-start a conversation with the sad, new soon-to-be owners of the mess we were trying to clean up.

"What is your name?" I asked hoping I would receive something other than a glaring stare in response.

"I'm Sarah and that's my husband, Mike. It's my mom and dad who are getting this house. It's a mess. I don't know how those Habitat people think we can live in a mess like this," she said sullenly.

There was no doubt that she and her husband were not happy. They weren't too anxious about attacking the mess that was strewn all through the house.

"I thought you said your mom and dad were going to live here. That doesn't matter because it will look just like new when we get finished. Don't worry about how it looks now."

"How can you make this mess disappear? How can anyone want to live here?"

"Why don't you guys start in the back bedroom? Sonny and I will do the kitchen and the living room. All we are required to do is clean up and splash on a few gallons of this cover-up paint. Habitat will make sure all major repair jobs are completed to your satisfaction or that of your mother and father. I'm sure by the time this place is finished, it will look like new."

"It can't possibly look new ever again," she said as she stomped out of the room and out the front door.

Sonny and I worked hard for long hours as we shoveled, swept, and then vacuumed the floors. I tackled the kitchen appliances that were caked with burnt on food and grime. The refrigerator was a disaster for the nose. Food had been allowed to remain inside when there was no electricity so all kinds of molds and fungi were spreading happily to cover every surface.

I crawled inside of cabinets wiping them clean while Sonny tackled closets and, once again, started loading up garbage bags.

The previous owners, it was rumored, had been involved with drugs. Part of the ceiling in one of the bedrooms was caving in where a person had climbed into the area to either hide himself or heavy containers of whatever your imagination allowed you to see. I was inclined to believe it was a human that was being hid from the legal authorities.

The walls, all of them, were covered with crayon, permanent marker, and nail polish child high. No amount of scrubbing and elbow grease was going to remove the destruction that was allowed to roam through the house in the form of neglected children. It would take more than one coat of cover up paint; several coats would be my guess.

It wasn't our house. We had our house. We were treating this house as if it were going to come into our hands so we worked very hard to make it presentable to the new owners.

This work was all volunteer, well not exactly all volunteer. We felt obligated to accomplish our goal but if we had been physically unable to do the job, we would not have been chastised in any way. We felt we needed to do this to thank the Stillwell County Habitat for Humanity for giving us a chance.

It took us a couple of weekends but when we were finished, all the new owners had to do was paint the walls the colors they preferred. Habitat had furnished new carpet and all of the repair work necessary to make the house like the new home that it was.

In my heart, I still find it difficult to understand why anyone would allow a brand new house to be destroyed like the previous owners had done. Also, I find it hard to understand how the family members of the new owners can be so critical and resentful of the golden opportunity to improve the family's living conditions when some hard work might be involved. You had to earn the right to own a Habitat House.

Sonny and I earned our right to own our house without resentment. We hoped that others would feel as we do and continue to work to earn their own houses and be grateful for the opportunity that had been given to them.

CHAPTER 16
ENOUGH OF THE MEMORIES

Enough of the memories, good and bad. Enough of watching scenes from my life pass before my eyes as if I was going to die at any moment.

That was not going to happen.

"Lady, I'm sure that was the same tunnel. Did you turn around?"

"Yes."

"I should kill you for that," he sputtered angrily.

"We're halfway back to Roanoke. I told you I had a sick husband," I answered back in an equally angry tone.

"Get off this interstate at the next exit," he snarled.

"If I do that, I'll get lost. I don't know my way around once I get off the interstate. I can get to and from the hospital. That's all I know, really," I said as I tried to make him understand my dilemma.

"I don't believe you, Lady."

"You'll be sorry, John. Most likely I'll be leading you into a trap out of sheer stupidity. Don't think that I didn't warn you. I can get lost in a brown paper bag. I truly have no sense of direction."

"You had enough sense of direction to get back to Roanoke, didn't you?" he snapped at me with glints like darts from his eyes.

"Yes. But I remained on the path that I know. All I did was turn around. Believe me, John, if I get off of the interstate, I'm lost."

"After what you've just pulled, there is no way I can believe you."

"I wish you would, John. I'm telling the truth."

"Turn here, this exit, now," he snapped as he pointed his finger toward the exit sign that was displayed before me.

I wasn't paying attention so I didn't have a clue as to where I was heading the car. *Was I driving toward a small town? Was I on the outskirts of Roanoke proper?*

No, I can't be. We haven't gone through the second tunnel. It must be just up ahead.

I had been too busy talking, trying to convince him that I didn't know my way around and now everything I said was true. I didn't know where I was and I didn't know where I was going.

I kept going from bad to worse.

I was in a rural area. The exit led me to a service station on the left, a sandwich shop on the right, and a cow pasture dead ahead.

"John, we are out in the middle of nowhere. Which way do I turn?" I said as I turned my head right to left and back again looking for someplace to go.

My mind was filling with panic.

"Oh, God," I prayed, "what do I do now?"

At the end of the exit ramp, I didn't know which way to turn. Straight was out of the question unless I wanted to go graze with the cattle.

Right or left? Which direction was going to lead me into more trouble? Trouble I didn't want and I didn't need. The only thing I wanted to do was to go home, take a shower, get fresh clothes, go back to the hospital, and watch my husband survive his heart attack, and related heart problems, congestive heart failure, and anything else that may crop up, simply because I wanted to be there.

I arrived at the bottom of the ramp.

"Which way, John? Which way do you want me to go?"

"That's entirely up to you, Ellen. We need to go away from the hospital, away from your home, and away from those people who are chasing me."

I looked at him with total, complete despair.

"Where is that? How do I get there, John? Where…." I could utter no more words for the moment. The lump in my throat and the tears rolling down my cheeks prevented me from asking any more questions.

I pulled over to the side of the road, put the car in park, and I cried at the bottom of the exit ramp. Thank God there were no cars behind me. Thank God it was an isolated area. But then again, if someone was behind me, maybe they might guess that I needed help. Maybe help would be there.

"All right, stop it, Lady. Stop with the tears before I get good and mad at you."

I snuffed back all the fear, despair, and anger, sucked it all in, held my chin up, and looked at John.

"Please let me go. You can have the car but please let me go. I want to go check on my husband."

"Shut up, Lady, and drive."

He wouldn't tell me which direction. I was afraid I was going to choose the wrong one, but I had to drive.

I turned right. I had no particular reason to turn right except that I was far over in the right lane and it was safer than trying to cross the ramp to make a left turn.

As I started to crawl along the road, he got irritated again.

"Speed it up."

"Okay."

I pushed my foot gently further into the gas pedal, increasing my speed slowly, until it got up to where I thought it should be. I had not seen a speed limit sign, but I knew there had to be one somewhere so I would keep my eyes peeled.

I saw a sign displaying the route number 636. Never heard of it. I don't know where it led and I didn't know what would happen when I got there.

I saw no signs indicating that there were towns of any kind ahead. That was good maybe. At least, it wasn't telling me that I was going back to Roanoke for the moment. If I was heading to Roanoke, I didn't want John to know it. If I was Roanoke bound, it was only by accident. He wouldn't understand that.

Why do my husband and I always lead such a solitary life?

Why don't we know more people?

Why didn't we become bosom buddies with someone that might worry about either one of us not being home? Most likely they would think Sonny was in the hospital and they would assume that I was with him. Boy, would they be wrong.

Gosh, I wished somebody missed me. I wished somebody would send out an army to find me. Just send somebody out to help me get out of this mess. I didn't know if anyone knew my vehicle license number or what car I drove. Those at work would know from a glance that it was mine, but to tell anybody what my specific vehicle license number was, the plate number, they wouldn't know. They probably wouldn't know what year my car was or, for that matter, what make or model. They would know the color. It was sort of a sand color, a wet sand color.

No one would be looking for me, I knew that.

My son wouldn't be because he expected me to be at the hospital. He worked crazy hours so he knew I didn't always get a chance to call him for fear of waking him from a sound sleep. It would take two or three days of mom not calling before he would really get nervous.

Maybe my friend Dreama would miss me. She might get worried enough to try to track me down at the hospital. She might send somebody in to ask Sonny where I was and to have him to tell me to call her. She would do that.

Maybe Donna would miss me but Donna had a busy life and it didn't always include worrying about me and Sonny. She did what she could. She was a nurse practitioner and had the worries of the entire community on her shoulders. We weren't the only people that would concern her. I really do feel lucky when I get a concerned phone call from her.

Here I am stuck next to – what should I call him? A kidnapper? A carjacker? A robber? A murderer, if the man dies that he shot?

What am I supposed to do?

Pray?

I didn't do that very well. Maybe I did. If I hadn't prayed in the past, my husband still wouldn't be alive, I was sure of that.

God had a reason to listen then. My husband was sick and I was trying to do the best I could.

Maybe God was just telling me it was my turn. I had gotten by with more than I should have. I had managed to keep my husband. The doctors had worked to keep away the Grim Reaper. The funeral had been put on hold for at least a few more days, hopefully a few months or years.

"God," I prayed, "help me get out of this. Tell me what I can do. I don't know what I can do."

I looked to the side at John and his head was bobbing with the flow of the car. He was sleeping or close to it. I knew he was extremely tired. I was, too. And, I was hungry.

"John."

"Huh, what?"

"I've got to go pee."

"You've got to what?"

"It's been a long time, John. I have to go pee. I'm an old lady, remember? Old ladies have to go often."

"Aw, Lady."

I could tell he was getting irritable and tired. I didn't want to push him too far.

"Can I stop at the next gas station to see if it has a restroom?"

"I'll let you know when we get there."

"Okay."

I wiggled around like I was in misery which, to tell you the truth, I was. I really did have to go pee.

I continued to drive, but now, I had a purpose. I was going to find a gas station. It was a fact of life.

"Lady?"

"Yes, John."

"Tell me about yourself."

"What do you want to know?"

"What it is you do?"

CHAPTER 17
WHAT CHOICE DID I HAVE?

I chose to tell him the story that Sonny told me about the dream he had one night between heart attacks…

He reached for the bottle. He needed a spritz, one little spray of the nitroglycerin. He had to have it to calm the pain that was building in his chest.

"Sixty years old is too young to be teetering towards death," he mumbled.

He had no idea when he was diagnosed with a heart condition at forty-five that he would spend so many days in doctors' offices and hospitals.

The money that was being spent to keep him alive was unbelievable.

His trembling hands crawled through the darkness toward his nightstand. He was shaking all over.

"What is happening to me?" he whispered, at least, he thought he said the words with his mouth and not his mind.

The room was so much darker than he could remember it ever being.

"The night light must have burned out," he said as he continued to extend his hand and arm reaching toward his nightstand.

"Where is it? It's supposed to be right next to my bed. All of my pills are in the drawer and the nitro is positioned on the top where I can get at it anytime I need it.

"Where is my lamp? I want to turn on a light to help me find the nitro," he said as he started to wave his arm and hand around in the dark air searching for the immediate help that he needed.

If he could find the nightstand, he could turn on the light and locate his nitroglycerin spray. If, after a dose or two of the spray he was still having the pain, he could grab the walkie-talkie he had next to the nitro and press the button summoning me, his wife, as I was sleeping in another room.

We hadn't slept in the same room for years because of all of his health problems.

He floundered around in bed and got up so much during the night that I wasn't able to get a good night's rest. That wasn't going to work because I had to keep my job to keep the insurance up and running for him.

It was hard on me because the years were piling onto my frame as rapidly as they piled onto his, but I had to do it. What choice did I have other than to let him die?

"Where is it? Why can't I find my night stand?" he screamed into the darkness as the pain worsened in his chest. "I did scream, didn't I? Why isn't she coming to help me?"

He pulled his arm in next to his body and willed himself to be quiet. He needed to know if the quiet would help him calm down and cause the pain to ease up.

"It is so dark. Why is it so dark?"

The pain seemed to lessen.

"Is it going to go away?" he asked the darkness.

He almost fell asleep. He jerked himself awake.

"Why can't I find my nightstand? Why can't I find my nitro? Why can't I find my lamp?" he whimpered softly.

"Maybe she's tired of me. Maybe she has decided it's time. I can't blame her for that, not one little bit. She has had to put her life on hold for years waiting for me to die. Has the time come?"

He shook his head from side to side. He had to push out those thoughts, never to think about them.

"It's so dark in here. Is this the way it is when you are dying? How much longer do I have? Does she still know that I love her? Does she know that I understand? I hope she does. I don't blame her."

He tried to sleep again.

"I thought there would be a bright light reaching out for me pulling me into its molten beauty. It is supposed to swallow me up and take me to higher ground among the stars and heavens.

"Oh no, I'm not going to heaven. Is that it? Is that why it's so dark in here?" he rubbed at his eyes.

"If I close my eyes will the bright light come? Will I go to heaven? I'm not ready to go yet. I thought I would be ready, but I'm not. Why did she move my nightstand?"

He thrashed around in his bed trying to fend off his angel of death.

Suddenly he felt a warmth creeping up his backside.

Then, it wasn't warm. It was cold and clammy because he had wet himself.

"What is wrong with me?" he cried as he tried to will himself to dry so that he wouldn't be embarrassed because someone had to change his bed linens.

He was going to lie there in the cold, wet bed until I came in to check on him.

"Maybe I'm dying. They say all of your systems stop functioning when you're getting ready to die. Maybe my kidneys are going to stop functioning. Is that the first system to go?"

He reached his arm up to his chest where he touched his breastbone above where his heart should be pumping.

"I guess my heart's still pumping. I wouldn't be moving my arm if it weren't."

Next, he checked to see if breath could be felt leaving his nostrils.

"Yeah, I'm still pushing out air," he said as he reached up to his eye where he poked himself in the eyeball. "God, that hurt. That was a stupid thing to do."

The urine was cold and making him shiver.

He reached out his arm again in search of his nightstand.

"It's there. I found it," he whispered loudly.

He moved his hand up and over to where he found his lamp and switched it on to light up his small room.

He reached for the walkie-talkie, pressed the button as he forced a tearful cry for me, his beloved wife of more than twenty years.

I didn't take the time to respond to the cry on the walk-talkie. I jumped from my bed and raced into Sonny's room.

"Sonny, are you okay?" I asked worriedly.

"Ellen, I wet the bed. I must have had a bad dream. I'm so sorry, Honey," he cried in explanation.

"You get up from there and I'll help you into the bathroom so you can change your clothes. Clean up the best you can for now. We'll do a better job of it tomorrow. I'll change your bed. You didn't get the mattress wet. Don't worry about that. Remember, we put rubber sheets on it for protection. We'll keep them on the bed until you get better, so don't worry."

"Okay, that's right. I forgot about the rubber sheets," he answered as I supported his average size frame while he shuffled his slippered feet towards the bathroom. He closed the door and looked into the mirror.

"She still loves me," he mumbled as he cleaned himself up with a hint of a smile on his aging face.

CHAPTER 18
HOUSE NOISES

"You love your husband very much. I can tell that from the way you talk about him."

"Yes, I do, but we have had our little spats. It wasn't wonderful all of the time…"

Suddenly the window slammed shut. It was a wonder the glass didn't shatter.

"What caused that?" I asked no one. I only want to hear the comfort of my own voice. Actually, I didn't know the window was open. It shouldn't be. It was winter time and Virginia was not Florida or California temperature wise.

Here I was, alone in this big old house. It was a mansion from by-gone days that had been transitioned into an office building to house the Stillwell County School Board Office.

"Why on Earth would anybody have the window open now?" I mumbled as I looked from room to room trying to locate the specific window.

I couldn't find the window.

Then, with a slap to the forehead with the heel of my hand, I realized that I might not be alone.

"Oh, my God!" I whispered as I started extinguishing lights so my possible night visitor wouldn't be able to follow my trail so easily.

Normally, this empty, rattily old house didn't bother me. Why now? Was it just the slamming window?

Why am I here?

I shouldn't have been here at all. I should have been at my house getting ready for bed in the cozy comfort of my home.

Dreama was the one who suggested I hide out here. *Why did I let her talk me into this?*

Of course, she was only trying to help. I knew that. I still loved her anyway. She was like the sister I never had.

I didn't have the money to rent a motel room and I certainly didn't want to drag my friends into my personal problems, so I had no other choice but to spend the night at the office.

I brought with me a couple of blankets and a pillow that I kept in the car and planned to curl up on the hard carpeted floor when the need arose. Until then, I would sit in my office and stare into the darkness, waiting for the hours to tick away.

I heard the house noises that I normally heard when I was here working alone. Nothing was different except that I was on alert.

I started to relax and get sleepy hoping that all was well.

I drifted off for a few moments as I laid my head on my crossed arms that were propped up by my desk top.

I was not quite into a sound sleep when I was startled by another loud noise. I blinked my eyes to become awake so that I could identify the intruder into my world of sleep.

"WHOoooo, WHOoooooo" followed by scratch, clatter, brush and "WHOoooo, WHOooo," whispered the wind as it sang its song to let me know that the outside world was nowhere near as calm as my inside world in my cozy office.

I had never heard the wind make such weird, frightening sounds, but I guessed there was a first time for everything. It seemed especially scary since I was here alone.

Late in the night, the weather forecast was calling for snow. An early snow fall was not what I needed. Snow would fall upon my depressingly, weary world. I hoped I wouldn't get snowed in, but it wouldn't matter. No one even knew I was here. As long as I could scramble around, scratch up some food to eat, I would survive. I was good at surviving.

Speaking of food, I was hungry. Maybe I could find a cookie or something along that line. I knew I had a couple of diet sodas in the refrigerator outside my office. I needed to go scrounging around for something to munch. I had to eat something to make me happy, to make me feel comfortable, and to make me feel like I should just go on living for now.

I crept down to the kitchen. It was my hope that someone had been kind enough to store some leftover crackers or cookies in the cupboards above the sink where my coworkers usually placed extra food for all to share.

I didn't want to turn on any lights. I really didn't need them, just in certain areas where there were no windows allowing any outside light available to filter inside or no office equipment with little shining lights coming from the surge protectors, buttons on computer screens, and buttons on printers. That sort of sounded funny, but they did provide enough light in a group in an office to let me get through a room without killing myself.

The kitchen had a window, but it was high up, and that was the only light in there except for a microwave clock that was on the other side of the refrigerator, so I really couldn't see it when I walked into the kitchen. All I could possibly see was a faint glow and that was about it for illumination in the kitchen without switching on the overhead fixture.

I had to take a chance to flash on a light really quick to see what was in the cupboard. Before I could do that, I heard a noise coming from the cupboard, I thought. I stopped in my tracks and I backed up.

"Naw, mice can't get up there. Couldn't be a mouse," I mumbled. "Couldn't be anything else except maybe a box falling over. How in the world could a mouse get up there?"

I decided I wasn't interested enough in the contents of the cupboard to continue to search for crackers and cookies.

"Maybe I'm not hungry after all. I'll drink a soda. Maybe that will kill the urge to eat. I don't know what that noise was, but I am not about to face it in the middle of the night," I said as I turned away from the kitchen. Talking to myself was a habit that had become well developed over the last few years. I knew I was destined to have many conversations with myself until the day I die. It seemed that I must hear certain words said out loud before I could take any action such as making a decision that might be important to me or my family.

I tried to enter the accounts payable office because occasionally they had some food sitting out on the counter in there. They didn't care if you ate it or not. It was there for everybody.

The door was locked. That was the first time the door had ever been locked

"When did they start locking it?" I whispered.

Of course, it had been a while since I was here late. I usually come in early and I never paid any attention to what was open and what was closed. Every morning I made the coffee, gathered in the newspapers, flipped the switches for all of the lights on the first floor, and then walked upstairs to start my work. It never occurred to me that the closed door might have been locked. There had been whispers about unwelcomed guests removing files, but I didn't know steps had been taken to correct the problem.

Oh, well, I wondered if that was why that door was locked.

I looked down underneath the door to see if I could see a light in there. I couldn't see anything other than a little glow, such as the weird light coming from a computer screen or again those little lights on printers and such. Not everybody turned off their equipment like I did. Maybe I was not supposed to, maybe it was not good for the equipment, but I couldn't see letting it run all night long when I wasn't here. It seemed like such a waste of energy.

I gave that door a once over. I touched it as though I thought it might open with my magic touch. Nothing happened. I turned and walked away wondering why the lock was there.

Was it there to keep me out?

Strange things were happening in this building, but I didn't know why.

I had been told by a couple of people I worked with on the sly that there were some changes being made. They didn't know who they would affect and why?

Speculation was a living, breathing entity in this office. If the dust settled and all was running smoothly, someone dreamed up a new problem and a whirlwind caused a new tornado of speculation.

Maybe they were giving my job to someone else. Maybe they were reassigning duties again. They did that about every five years. They gave you more work but they didn't give you any more money.

My feeling was that once a purchase order clerk, always a purchase order clerk with extra duties. I was truly glad that I was also a writer. I needed to keep my mind active and repetitious entry of purchase orders was mind numbing, but writing kept me going.

I climbed the stairs, opened a can of soda pop, and sat in the darkness - listening. *Why was I listening? Why were my nerves on edge? Why was there a sound in the cupboard? Why was the door locked?*

I listened and I strained, wondering if I was going to make it through the night. It seemed like there was a problem, but I didn't know what the problem was.

I had my head down on the desk trying to sleep. I thought that would be a little better than being flat down on the floor on the blanket and pillow that I brought. I was afraid I might go too soundly asleep if I got comfortable. Forget that, there was no chance of me getting comfortable. That was all a pipe dream. A hard floor and fifty-eight-year old bones were not a good match.

I heard something. It sounded like something or someone was walking down the hall.

This was an old house that had been reformatted into an office building. I guessed it was good and sizeable at the beginning, but the number of people had grown and multiplied and the office space had shrunk. It was still an old building and the wooden floors did creak.

If that was a mouse, that was one *big* mouse to make the floor creak that loudly.

I was as motionless as I could be, I didn't even want to breathe. I was afraid he, she, or whatever would hear me. I wanted to know who was coming and why?

He didn't turn on the lights that would illuminate the world's doom and gloom in which I was trying to hide.

Suddenly the silence was overwhelming and I heard no more creaks, no more floor boards, nothing to make me think that my world was being invaded.

What happened? Where did he go? Is it a he?

My mind was filling in the blanks of huge proportions of murder, death, and destruction. None of which I hoped was true, but then, who knew? Maybe it was my writer's mind being too active.

I slid my chair back and rose to my feet again.

"This is getting old," I mumbled.

I needed to go downstairs and check the first floor again. I might even need to check the basement. I hadn't been down there to look to see if that door was locked. Occasionally someone left it unlocked, not often, but if anybody knew it was there and open, he could get in.

A fifty-eight-year old, two-hundred pound female trying to sneak surreptitiously down a hallway in the dark had to be a funny scene for the eyes of one watching the scenario that was unfolding.

What am I going to do except explore and look to see what is going on?

Is it the old house just settling down for the night, creaking and rattling like my old bones do on occasion?

I didn't think so. I had been here before at night so I knew it didn't make that much noise.

What is it?

I looked around my office before going into the hallway to find something to use as a weapon. I didn't see anything. *What can I use?*

A pair of scissors? Yeah, they were just as dangerous to me as they were to an attacker. They were long, sharp pointed things that I'd had for sixteen years. They were deadly weapons as far as I was concerned.

They might be needed, so I slid open the desk drawer, searched in the dark, feeling around with my hand and fingers trying to find the loops of the handle of the dangerous scissors.

With scissors in hand, I started walking forward to find out why I was so scared. *What is bothering me?*

That was when I heard it.

Tap-Tap-Tap.

I stopped in my tracks. I didn't know whether to go forward or backward. *Should I run into my office, lock the door, or run out, down the hall, down the stairs to reach the front door or the back door. Which one?*

I didn't know where the tapping was coming from.

193

What is that tapping? Is somebody knocking at the door? Why would they be knocking at the door at this time of night? Then again, why am I here at this time of night?

I stood in place straining to hear the tapping. It wasn't loud. It wasn't a banging sound. I was guessing that it was not an angry person. Maybe it was someone checking to see if anybody was here. Maybe it was the sheriff. Maybe he saw a figure floating around inside the building, a glimpse of me moving or perhaps it was something else or someone else, and he wasn't sure if anybody was there or not. So, he was tapping at the door to see if it was an employee.

Then again, maybe it was a serial killer, or a rapist, or a murderer, or an escaped convict. It could be any number of things. I didn't want to be the one who opened the door to the shooting gun, or the slashing knife, or the sudden attack from a rapist.

I spun myself around three hundred sixty degrees slowly as I tried to figure out from which direction the tapping was coming.

It sounded like somebody was knocking at the door. *Which door?*

This place had one – two – three – four - five doors to the outside on the first floor. There was a door to the outside on each of the second and third floors accessed by wooden steps. And, of course, there was the basement door. It was really hard to determine which door was being tapped.

I strained with all of my might to listen to find out from what direction the tapping was being done.

I thought I had figured it out.

It sounded like it was at the other end of the hall, close to the staircase, and on the first floor. That meant it was the door that three-fourths of the people that worked here used. That would also mean that the tapper had to be familiar with the ins and outs of the building to know that it was the entrance that was used all of the time by the employees.

Maybe I was safe. Maybe it was just someone who worked here. Maybe it was just the sheriff checking for movement in the building.

I moved forward, listening and straining with every step. I got to the steps and hoped that I could walk down the steps without the wooden structures creaking too much. The steps were the center piece of the building. They were off the foyer as you came into the building which was now an office for the receptionist. As soon as you entered the building, you faced the stairway that led up to a landing with another set of stairs behind a door that went up to the third floor. Two more sets of stairs curved to the right and left that continued on to the second floor off of the landing.

It was a beautiful staircase and in the winter time Nellie decorated it to showpiece status. We were all proud of the staircase, except me right at this moment. I was not proud because sometimes the boards creaked when I tread on them. I did not want that noise to happen. I didn't know where the person who was tapping was standing. Perhaps that person was already inside and tapping on the door to attract my attention and get me downstairs.

I slowly made each step, praying that my two-hundred pound weight wouldn't make the boards creak. The boards were uncarpeted with no runner of any type, so if they were going to creak, there was nothing to muffle them.

Slowly I slipped down the steps one at a time. I got to the bottom and I didn't hear the tapping. I didn't see any movement. Nothing was disturbed downstairs.

"He must be outside," I whispered.

I walked to the back door where I thought the tapping was coming from and I stood in front of it hoping there wouldn't be a gunshot blast tearing through the wooden panels.

I heard the tap-tap-tap right in front of me.

I jumped as if the gun shot did come through the door.

What should I do? Should I open that door?

Maybe I can pull the curtain back just a little to see who is out there. Is it anybody I know? Should I let him in, or not?

I walked as close to the door as I could and tugged at the curtain. I peeked through it.

A dark shadow, nothing else, was all I could see.

The light was shining from behind the figure silhouetting the body making the form entirely dark in front of me. It was a man. The body was familiar. It was somebody I knew.

"Dear Lord, it's time for me to open this door and find out what's going on."

I turned the lock and the body jumped at me.

"Ellen, what are you doing in there?"

"I'm hiding, Sonny. I'm hiding."

"What are you hiding from?"

"You."

"Why?"

"If you haven't figured it out, I'm mad at you."

"Why?"

"Where were you today?"

"I was over at the camp digging holes and planting stuff for the opening of the camp for the handicapped children."

"Were you supposed to be doing that?"

"Well, no."

"Then why are you doing it?"

"They need help."

"They can get their help from somebody else. You've got a heart condition. You don't need to be doing that."

"So, why are you gone?"

"You need something to worry about, Sonny. If I wasn't home and you couldn't find me, maybe you would worry about me for a while. I'm very tired and worn out from worrying about you."

"Aw, Ellen."

"I mean it, Sonny. That type of work can cause you to have another heart attack. The doctor told you not to do anything like that. If you continue to do that, I'm going to be gone."

"You wouldn't leave me."

"Hide and watch, Sonny. I can't constantly be worrying about you doing something stupid," I explained knowing that I would worry about him if I were gone.

"Come on home, Ellen."

"Why?"

"I promise not to do anything stupid. I promise to do what the doctor says. I take the pills. I do everything I'm told except that I was digging in the dirt over at the camp."

"That puts a strain on your heart and you've had open heart surgery. You have twenty plus stents in your heart right now. We have gone through trip after trip out of town to the hospitals. You need to be smart about living out the rest of your life, if you want to do that."

"Of course, I want to do that, Ellen. Please come home."

"Okay, I'll go get my handbag. You stay here. I don't want you climbing the steps."

I walked upstairs to get my pillow, blanket, and handbag, and then I walked to the car.

After climbing into the vehicle, I gave him a big hug. I knew I had worried him, but I really had to do it.

"Why did you hide at the office, Ellen?"

"I didn't have any place else to go."

"You could have gone to Eddy's."

"I'm not going to pull Eddy into this. It's our argument, not his. Why would I pull my son into the middle of a mess?"

"You wouldn't do that. I know that."

"I just didn't have any other place to go. I didn't have the money to go spend it at a motel. I wasn't going to impose on any of my friends. So, where else would I go?"

"You've got a point. What made you change your mind so easily? I thought you would put up a big fight?"

I looked at him and smiled because I didn't want to tell him that I managed to scare myself using the writer's imagination that I have developed to its fullest extent.

"You can bring me back here tomorrow morning. We will just leave my car here overnight. Let's get out of here. This place was getting on my nerves. I spend all day in it. I don't want to spend all night in it. This old house is noisy and rattling and I'm hungry."

He laughed and drove to the house.

During the night, I checked on Sonny to make sure he was still breathing. I was glad I was home. I lived in constant fear that my husband might die. I didn't need the additional fear of staying in a creaky old house and being scared to death.

It was nice to be home.

CHAPTER 19
FOUR LARGE EGGS

"I'm good at surviving, John. No brag involved with that statement, only fact. No amount of knocking me to my knees will make me stay down. Life has been sort of rough going, but I'm still going," I said as I tried to display a hint of a smile.

"What has caused you to hone your survival skills? You work for a school system, don't you? Aren't you a teacher?"

"No, I'm not a teacher. I am a purchase order clerk which makes me a classified employee and as a classified employee I'm considered a step or two just above dirt in the eyes of some of those I work with who were fortunate enough to get their bought and paid for degree," I said in angry answer to his stupid question.

"I'm sorry, Lady, I just assumed you were a teacher," he sputtered in an apologetic tone.

"Don't be sorry, you aren't one of those who think I'm stupid because I don't have a degree. As a matter of fact, I've done something with my life that I'm sure ninety-nine percent of those degreed wonders of my world can't do."

"What would that be?"

"I wrote a book. It was actually published and I'm supposed to be out on the book circuit trying to sell it, but my plans had to be scrapped because my husband is so sick."

"Is that why you think you're so good at surviving?"

"That's part of it. I've had to survive on a dozen eggs for almost two weeks. Do you want to hear that tale of woe?"

He nodded and I began…

Four large eggs are all that I had left between me and starvation.

I looked inside my refrigerator and saw them cradled in their cardboard carton enticing me to delve into their delicate texture and taste.

I can't. I have already eaten my eggs for the day. I must wait until tomorrow to be able to eat two more.

It wasn't heart problems that prevented me from eating the eggs and the cholesterol building numerical figure that many people were faced with nowadays. What kept me from eating those eggs was that I had nothing else to eat tomorrow if I ate them today. It was the same set of circumstances for the next day. I knew I had a meal of two fried eggs for each day. After that, the job prospect for which I had already interviewed would come through, I hoped.

What do you do when you have no food and you have no money?

At least, I had a place to live the next few days. It was a small house for which I had taken over the rent payment from my brother after he moved out and into his girlfriend's home. I did have a place to go if I didn't mind starving to death.

It was time for my daily walk to scour the trashcans for newspapers. Most people, when finished with their daily reading, would give the newspaper a toss and that was what I was counting on. I needed to find out if there was anything available for an almost starving woman.

I kept in mind that I had four large eggs.

My brother's phone was still connected and, of course, it was in his name. I begged him to let me keep it until I could find a job at which time he could take it out of his name and I would get it transferred to my name. That was my hope.

At the rate things were going, my hope was nothing more than a pipe dream.

The only job I was able to find that looked the least bit interesting was with a CB radio warehouse. Mr. Owens was the man who talked to me. He seemed encouraging. I told him I had seen his ad in the newspaper and I was willing to work for anything, minimum wage, if nothing else, so that I could get my feet wet again after pulling up stakes three months earlier and moving two hundred fifty miles south.

I moved south to be with my parents, especially my dad because of his failing health. Dad passed on and mom finally settled and accepted dad's death and was now able to carry on.

I moved out searching for a life where I could start over.

When I left mom, I had enough money to pay for one month's rent in this little house and forty dollars for gas money; twenty to get to where I am now and twenty to get back to live with mom if all else failed.

I didn't want to fail. I wanted to stay right where I was and resume my life as it was before my dad became seriously ill.

Time was running out. I didn't know what I was going to do.

I strolled along the street lifting the tops off of the protected trashcans and peered inside looking for a newspaper. I could find everything but what I wanted in that trash can. I walked on to the next one. I ripped the top off of it and stared down at a neatly folded today's date newspaper.

I grabbed it up only to discover that folded neatly inside of it is somebody's vomit.

"Yuck!!" I shouted as I threw it back into the trashcan.

I continued walking to the next trashcan where at the bottom of it is another newspaper that has been basically pulled from its folds but it was still intact meaning that it looked as though the classified section was there. That was what I needed, the classified section, just in case my job interview failed me.

I was never good on job interviews but I thought he was willing to hire me. I hoped he would. I didn't want to wander too far out on the street. I had to go back to be near the phone between eight and five to await that phone call. The only reason I was out now was that it was lunch time and I was assuming he would eat lunch between twelve and one so that I could go newspaper searching.

I walked back to the house where I sat on my sofa and stared at the telephone that wasn't ringing.

With each passing moment, the tension was building up and the stress level was making me so hungry that I wanted to attack the refrigerator and fry me a couple more eggs. I was hungry. I had spent four days already surviving on two eggs per day. I thought my body should have adjusted to the fact that I was only getting two eggs per day. It wasn't adjusting and I was hungry.

I counted the seconds down because my goal was to sit there until five o'clock when I knew his work hours ended at Commtron. Then, I was going to go search those very same trashcans for a couple of morsels of food that looked like they were fit to eat without causing me to die from some deadly contagion. I focused my mind on what was comically known as dumpster diving for food.

At about two minutes before five I rose from the sofa and started moving around.

The phone rang.

"Oh, my God, the phone. Please let it be him," I prayed.

I plucked the receiver from its cradle.

"Hello?"

"Miss Hutchins, this is Tim Owens from Commtron."

"Oh, hi, Mr. Owens."

"I'm calling to see when you will be able to come to work. We want to hire you. It will be minimum wage and it will be part time. We'll see how things work out. If everything goes well, we'll change it to full time and give you a little more money."

"That's great, Mr. Owens, when can I start?"

"Tomorrow. Can you come in tomorrow?"

"Yes, Sir, I can. Mr. Owens, thank you, thank you so much."

The need for food suddenly left me. All I can do was smile and say, "Thank you, thank you, God, thank you."

It was hard to sleep because I was much too excited. I rose bright and early to get ready to drive to my new found job. I had to drive because I couldn't take a bus. Reason number one for driving was that I didn't know how to get to Commtron on a bus. The second reason was that I didn't think I could scratch up the money to put into the fare box when I knew I had enough gas in my car to get me to and from work for a couple of days.

The job Tim hired me for is to be a file clerk to straighten out some extremely awful customer files that a person who has never filed before had totally discombobulated.

"Ellen, you know how to file, right?"

"Yes, Sir. You asked me that when we first talked."

"Good. That's what you will be doing for a while. I cannot find anything. If a customer has a question or a complaint, it takes me a good three days to find the file. Please start with that file cabinet and begin with the letter "A." Don't just assume that what's in there is right because what's in there is wrong. You'll have to go from A to Z, fresh and new."

"Yes, Sir."

I worked, the lunch hour arrived, and I didn't leave.

"Ellen, aren't you going to lunch?"

"No, Sir, I thought I'd just stay here."

"Well, I'm going to go. You want me to bring you something back?"

"No, Sir, I don't – no, I'm not hungry."

"What is it you like, Ellen? Do you like hamburgers? I'll bring you a hamburger."

"Thank you, Sir."

He left for lunch and I wanted to cry. He must have guessed that I didn't have any money for food.

My stomach was making mild, rumbling noises due to hunger the entire time he was gone. As soon as he arrived, I snatched the bag he handed to me, ripped it open, and tried to make myself eat slowly to savor every morsel. I didn't know when I would get to eat again. I didn't know when I would get paid. It was only Wednesday.

He watched me and he knew I was hungry. He walked to the soda machine and purchased a cold drink that he handed to me.

"Haven't had much to eat for a while, have you, Ellen?"

"No, but now that I'm working, I will survive."

"What about you, John? This is a two-way street, you know. Tell me something about you," I said as I tried to get him to let me in on what might be lying ahead of me.

"No, not now, maybe later. You go on about your life. What makes you an exceptional survivor?" he asked as he stifled a yawn.

"I want to know something about you, John. Why did you rob that bank?"

"I told you before that I needed the money."

"Why?"

"To pay bills."

"What kind of bills?"

"Medical for my mom and her funeral. She isn't dead yet, but she will be soon. I've lost my job, my car, and everything else. All I wanted to do was get enough money to pay some bills."

"I'm sorry, John, about your mother and robbing a bank wasn't the answer, was it?"

"It's the only answer I could think of. I really didn't mean to shoot that guard. Now, I am done talking," he said as he yawned again.

I hoped he wasn't going to even think about locking me in the trunk again so he could get some sleep. It was best to keep him listening and awake for the time being.

"You wanted to know why I was good at surviving. Well, the husband that I'm so worried about, John, is my third husband. The first two were mistakes. This third husband, Sonny, is all right. It took me two practice tries to get the right one. I don't want to lose him, John. We've been married for what will soon be twenty-four years. Now, you can see why I'm worried about him, can't you?"

"Sure, Lady, sure, I know you're worried about him. What about the first two husbands? What happened to them?" he asked as he tried to hide another yawn.

"Husband number one fathered my two sons. I will always be grateful that I have my boys. Unfortunately, I had to be married to their father to get them."

"Why was he a bad choice?"

"He liked to drink and chase other women. It sort of made me mad when he did that, you know?"

"Yeah, I guess it would."

"Of course, I'm not the easiest person in the world to live with and when I get something set in my mind, it's hard to shake it out of my head."

"What does that mean?"

"He started chasing my best friend trying to get her into the sack. I really think he accomplished that but neither one of them would admit it. My gut told me they were a thing for quite a while. I really didn't know who to blame for that. Her, for allowing him to do it? Or him, for going after my best friend? Either way, I didn't like it one bit. So I told him to get out of my life."

"Did he go?"

"Not without a fight. My family was mad at me because I wanted a divorce. His family was mad at me because I was telling everybody I didn't love him anymore. I didn't want to go into detail. I didn't want to tell everybody that he was bedding other women. I especially didn't want to tell anybody that he was abusing his eldest son. He couldn't get by with hurting the baby, but he did bang around on Eddy some. He actually left bruises on him that I lied about just to keep him out of trouble."

"Doesn't sound like a marriage made in heaven."

"No, it wasn't. Took me five years to get away from that loser and then I had to struggle along for eight years as a single mother before I succumbed to the marriage virus again. Then husband number two entered my life."

"Was he a drinker and woman chaser, too?"

"Mike was different. He was a divorced man with two daughters that were the same age as my two sons. All of the kids promised to get along but that didn't happen. My eldest and his eldest were like oil and water. They didn't even try to get along. I was made to be the heavy in the picture with Mike refusing to take part in any discipline of his daughters.

"I tired of that situation quickly and within six months I had typed and filed my own marriage dissolution in court.

"Mike was a good man, but he was making me live the life of the wicked stepmother. I didn't like that, not one little bit."

I glanced at John and saw that his head was bobbing up and down with the motion of the car.

I spotted a rest area and pulled the car into the parking slot as smoothly as I could.

I reached for the door handle.

"Where do you think you're going?" he demanded.

"To the women's restroom. I told you a while back that I needed to pee."

"I've got this gun and I will use it again. So make it quick," he snarled as he waved the gun at me below window level.

I was sure he had to go to the men's room, but he wasn't going to tell me. He was going to wait until I go inside and I wouldn't be able to see that he couldn't keep the gun trained on the bathroom door.

I grabbed a tube of lipstick from my handbag. I shoved the tube into my pocket. Let him think I was so vain that I had to primp and make my lips fresh even as I was being carjacked.

"Don't take a long time in there. I'll come get you if I have to."

"I have to take a dump, my stomach is cramping," I said as I squirmed in my seat.

"A dump? You work for a school system. Shouldn't you say it more politely?"

"Would you prefer that I take a sh…"

"No, no, I get the picture. Just hurry up," he said as he interrupted my question.

It struck me as odd that he didn't want me to say the "s" word. Maybe he wasn't such a bad guy.

If only I can get away? I don't want him to have to prove to me that he can be bad.

CHAPTER 20
I HAVE BEEN CARJACKED

The women's restroom was completely empty of human occupants except for me. I entered a stall, unbuttoned my pants, and seated myself for the performance of the necessary biological function. Then, I started writing on the bathroom wall with the tube of lipstick I shoved into my pocket.

> My name is Ellen Holcombe.
> I have been carjacked.
> My license number is YMS3304.
> Please help me.

The last few words were smeared badly. I was running out of writing instrument.

I used a finger to smear some fresh color to my lips so he wouldn't question my need to carry the tube of vanity into the restroom.

"Ellen, let's go!" bellowed the angry voice at the door.

"Okay, okay," I answered sullenly.

The door was yanked open and in he walked.

I was standing at the sink washing my hands and glancing at my reflection in the mirror.

John pushed on each stall door checking the inside of each cubicle.

As he was looking at stall walls, I ran out the restroom door.

I couldn't go to the car. I knew I couldn't get inside, start the car, and leave before he got to me.

I ran behind the rest area making sure to stay on the grass so that my shoes hitting the concrete and gravel of the walkway couldn't be heard.

I didn't hear him chasing me or calling my name. Then, I realized why.

He was cleaning my words off the ladies' room stall wall. He couldn't allow anyone to read it. It would be too dangerous.

The first attempt at leaving a message in the ladies' bathroom had produced no results. Why on Earth did I think a second message would bring me some positive results?

I stopped to get a breath. This old lady was out of shape and now it was really beginning to show.

I was about to enter an area that was heavily wooded. I know there had to be a fence somewhere that I would have to climb over somehow. There was always a fence surrounding the rest areas.

The daylight was fading and the path I was trying to blaze was becoming fainter. Therefore, the fence will be harder to locate. This was state-owned property that I was standing on; there had to be a fence.

"Stop it, Ellen. Stop it right now!" I whispered harshly. "You're obsessing about a fence."

I didn't hear him coming after me. Surely he had removed all of those words by now. If he didn't get the wall spotless, he already had plenty of time to smear the lipsticked words beyond readability.

He wasn't coming after me.

Why?

Am I disappointed? Am I relieved? What is wrong with me?

Why isn't he chasing me?

I touched my thigh and felt the keys to the car. He didn't take them away from me before I entered the women's restroom. Big mistake for him because he couldn't jump into the car and leave.

The big mistake for me was that I couldn't jump in the car and leave. He would be waiting for me to do just that.

I continued my trek away from the parking lot, away from my car, towards the unknown.

I found the fence that was merely a rectangular shaped wire mesh. I stuck my foot into one of the rectangles, feeling that it was secure enough to hold my weight, then I proceeded to slowly take steps up the fence in the same fashion.

Up and over, that was easy enough.

Getting away and getting help was not going to be easy. Not easy at all.

I walked and walked and walked. I was climbing up the rolling hills and pastures of isolated farm land and descending into the valleys where I tried to avoid confrontations with the roaming cattle.

I was walking toward the mountain ridge with the thought in mind that I should be able to find a farm house or, at the very least, a paved road.

I was so hungry and tired but I had to keep going. It was dark and only the moonlight, what little there was of it, was lighting my path in my race away from my captor.

Lights up ahead.

A road.

Is it safe? Should I hide?

I was tired and hungry. I was too old for this. All I wanted to do was go see my husband.

I froze in my tracks as I willed myself to disappear.

"Ma'am," shouted a male voice. "Do you need any help?"

I spun around facing the two bright headlights shining on me.

"Yes, Sir, I surely do. I'm lost and I can't find my way back to my car."

The state police officer escorted me to his vehicle and helped guide me inside it to the back seat behind the wire mesh that protected the officer from dangerous people like me.

I felt like a prisoner, the guilty person, not the victim.

I guessed that was why I made the decision not to tell the officer about John.

I didn't really know for sure except that I didn't want to cause him more trouble. I made up my mind that I would get my son to go with me back to the rest area on the pretense that I had lost my keys.

CHAPTER 21
IT HAPPENED

"Eddy, I need your help," I said softly into the telephone because I knew I had woken him from a sound sleep.

"What? Mom, is that you?" he said as he tried to focus his thoughts on the telephone.

"Yes, Baby, it's me. I'm at the State Police Station in Wytheville. I need you to drive me to the rest stop between the two tunnels on Interstate 77 so I can pick up my car."

"Why is your car there? Why are you at a police station?"

"I'll explain all of that to you when you pick me up. Today is your day off, isn't it?"

"Yeah."

"Good, I don't want you to have to miss work. I'll give you some gas money."

"I don't care about the gas money. What is happening? Where is Sonny? Is he all right?"

"Yeah, I guess he's all right, but I'll explain everything when you get here."

"Okay, Mom, I'll call your cell when I'm ready to leave."

"Don't bother. It's in the car. I love you, Honey," I whispered because I was very near tears. This past couple of days had almost been more than I could bear.

I found a comfortable chair at the state police headquarters and settled down for a restful wait.

I tried to commit to memory for future reference the tale I had related to my interrogator about why I was on foot.

When asked about why I was walking, I had to come up with a quick answer. Truth or fiction, it was a story I had to remember.

"He wanted to push a simple dinner date into a memorable occasion. I wasn't willing to go that far. Anyway, I really didn't feel it was a date at all because we knew each other from work; or, that I was obligated to pay for it with a tumble in the back seat. I'm getting too old for that kind of teenage fun. I don't feel like entering my second childhood; not yet anyway. I think I've got a few more years before that happens. My husband and I can go hand in hand to senility."

That was it. That was what I told them. It did happen to me in the past. I recounted the old story and stayed away from the real truth. That was not what I would tell my son.

I slept.

"Mom, are you all right?"

"Yeah, Eddy. I just need to get to my car. Before I do that, stop at McDonald's. I see the sign over there. I'm so hungry. Do you have some money? My handbag is in the car."

"Yes, sure, Mom. What do you want to eat?"

"Anything. I know. Get two double cheeseburgers and two McChickens and we can each eat one of each. Get me a large Diet Coke. I'll give the money back to you when we get to the car."

"When was the last time you ate, Mom?"

"Couple of days ago."

"Why?"

"I'll explain as we go get the car. I promise."

I thanked the state police officer and left with my son.

I knew the officer must have thought I was a crazy old lady, but that was okay. Just as long as they believed my tale of woe.

I gulped down the food and pressed my son to hurry so I could get to my car.

"Okay, Mom, we're on our way. Now, tell me what happened?"

"What I'm going to tell you is for your ears only. I didn't tell the cops and I don't want you to tell them. Do you understand me?"

"Yes, okay, what happened?" he said angrily.

"I was carjacked in the Roanoke Hospital parking garage. I was held at gun point for two days and forced to drive wherever John told me to go."

"You're calling a kidnapper by his first name?"

"No, no, that was the name I gave him. I don't really know his name."

"How did this happen?"

"I was leaving the hospital to go home and check on the house and the animals. I needed a break from the antiseptic world I had been forced to live in while Sonny was recuperating from his health or heart problems."

"What next?"

"Well, I got in the car and all was well, I thought. Soon, I heard a noise and when I stopped to investigate, he jumped out of my trunk. I had no idea he was in there, hiding, waiting for me to drive him to safety. He had robbed a bank where he shot a man and he needed a safe way out of town. I wasn't going to argue with him. Remember, I told you he just shot a man. We drove until he got tired and then he locked me in the trunk of the car."

"How did you get away?"

"I kept driving in circles until I stopped at the rest area we're going to. Then I ran. I had the car keys in my pocket so he couldn't take the car. I was afraid to go to the car while he was still there. So, I ran until I could find help."

"Why didn't you tell the cops what happened? The truth, Mom, why didn't you tell then the truth?"

"I don't know except that I think John didn't mean to shoot anybody. He could have hurt me, but he didn't. You don't have a newspaper, do you?"

"No, I didn't know you needed one."

"I don't need one. I want to see if I can spot anything in there about a bank robbery. I want to see if they caught John. I really want to know who he is. Why he robbed that bank? I want to know if the guard died."

"Mom, do you have feelings for this man?"

"No, I'm just interested, that's all. I spent two days with him. He could have killed me several times over, but he didn't."

"What is it called when a victim sympathizes with the criminal? You know what I'm talking about. That Hearst girl had it when she was taken. I read about it. What's that called?"

"Stockholm Syndrome."

"Is that what's happening to you, Mom?"

"No, no, like I said. I don't think he meant for any of this to happen."

"Did he tell you that?"

"Yes."

"Why did you believe him?"

"Because he could have killed me. I gave him plenty of reasons to do it. I wouldn't shut up talking. You know how I am when I'm nervous."

The remainder of the ride was quiet. No more interrogations or accusations from Eddy.

"Here, that's the rest stop, up ahead. It says its two miles away. You need to pull in there and stay in the car until I have a look around. I don't think he will be there, but I don't know for sure."

"This is stupid, Mom. You should have told the cops," he said in a voice tinged with fear.

"I know, I know. Just do as I ask."

He spotted my car and made a beeline to park beside it.

"No, no, Eddy. Don't get too close."

"Why not?" he asked as he stomped on the brakes.

"I don't know if he's here watching the car. I need to look around a bit."

"Okay, okay, but this cloak and dagger stuff is getting on my nerves, Mom."

"Why don't you just let me out and go on your way. I have my keys and I want to check the place out before I climb into the car. I think it would be safer that way for both of us."

"Aw, Mom, don't be such a drama queen. I'm not going anywhere until you get into your car. Then, I'm going to follow you home. That's the way it's going to be so don't be trying to get me to leave without you."

"Okay, Baby, I'm sorry. I just don't want you to get hurt."

"I thought you said John was a nice guy."

"He is but he has been backed into a corner. He can't be nice anymore and survive. I'm afraid he will react like a caged animal and strike out to hurt anyone that comes near him."

We sat for a few minutes to observe. Nothing looked out of the ordinary. No one was lurking in the bushes or behind trees.

I exited Eddy's car and walked slowly to my vehicle expecting a mad man to come out of nowhere and grab me as he forced the hard metal gun barrel into my ribs.

I unlocked the car door, jumped into the car, started it up, and backed out of the parking space. I drove to my son's car where I shouted to him to go home. My plan was to go back to the hospital and see how my husband was doing.

I didn't know whether I should be happy or sad that John wasn't there at the rest area waiting for me to return.

I really needed to see my husband.

I really needed to see a newspaper.

I really needed to know why John robbed a bank.

I really needed to know if John was okay.

Above all, I really needed to know why I was still alive.

My gas tank was running low so I pulled off the interstate to find a gas station. I used my gas credit card to fill up the tank and buy a snack or two, a drink, and a newspaper.

The headline reads,

BANK ROBBER KILLED ON I-77

"Oh no," I muttered as I tried to read the story.

Alledged bank robber, John Sullivan, refused to give himself up in confrontation with the State Police along Interstate 77 last evening.

While on a routine inspection, State Police Officer James Parsons encountered a male pedestrian walking along I-77 where pedestrian traffic is not permitted for safety reasons.

Officer Parsons slowed to allow Sullivan to stop moving so the patrol car could pull to the side of the road.

While the patrol car was coming to a complete stop, Sullivan started running toward the wooded area beyond the gravel berm.

Officer Parsons drew his weapon and fired a warning shot to try to halt the progress of Sullivan.

Sullivan turned and fired at the law
enforcement officer causing the officer to
return fire with a shot that killed John
Sullivan.
The investigation continues and when new
information is uncovered, this newspaper
will furnish the news to you as soon as
possible.

Nothing was said about why John Sullivan robbed a
bank. Nothing was said to make him seem like a real live
human being suffering from a tremendous bout with bad
luck.

He was the "killer", a vicious animal, the scum of
life, the evil that had been eradicated by the goodness of a
clean shot from the gun of a law enforcement officer.

"John Sullivan didn't deserve to die," I mumbled as
tears streamed down my cheeks. "The guard didn't deserve
to die. I didn't deserve to be held at gunpoint for two days,
but it happened."

I drove towards Roanoke and to finally see how my
husband was surviving the implant of another stent in his
severely weakened heart.

CHAPTER 22
BACK TO THE HOSPITAL - FINALLY

When I arrived at the hospital, I was dressed in the same, now disheveled, dirty clothes that I was wearing when I left to check on the house.

I walked through the lobby and raced to the ladies' restroom so I could wash my face, comb my hair, and try to be a little more presentable than I guessed that I was.

The cold water on my face did wonders for my mood. It felt wonderful and I was ready to face my husband and the world.

I walked off the elevator into Room 835 where he had been when I left to check on the house.

The bed was empty and cleaned like it would be if someone was discharged from the hospital.

Panic engulfed me.

I stood and stared at the empty bed.

It never occurred to me to check with the information desk that I walked past on the first floor to find out where Sonny might be.

He couldn't have been discharged because I was the one who had to take him home.

I finally turned away from the empty bed and made my way to the nurses' station.

"Where is Sonny Holcombe?"

"Who are you?" demanded a gruff sounding nurse as she moved her eyes up and down my body checking out my messy appearance.

"I'm his wife," I snapped back at her obvious disapproval.

"CCU, he was moved to CCU after the stent was placed in his heart. That's on the seventh floor."

"Why?"

"You need to ask the doctor, Ma'am. I can't answer that," she said as she turned away from me to continue with her task at hand.

I entered the elevator to travel one floor down. Upon stepping off the elevator car, I turned right where I spotted an empty desk on which there were two telephones and a sign telling me to call the Cardiac Care Unit before entering.

Well, I did as I was instructed.

"This is Ellen Holcombe. My husband is Sonny Holcombe. Is it all right for me to visit him and what room is he in?"

"Hold on a moment. I'll check with his nurse."

The noises I heard after she laid the phone down without pushing the hold button were frightening.

"I think he is going to code, get me some help in here," was a muffled plea for help that I overheard over the telephone lines two sets of double doors away from the CCU.

Another muffled utterance, "Get the doctor, Mr. Holcombe is going into shock," was the statement I thought I heard. I thought the person said "Mr. Holcombe" but it was so muffled and distant sounding.

"Hello, talk to me, hello, hello," I shouted into the telephone but it was to no avail. When the person that answered my call laid the phone down to get Sonny's nurse to speak to me, I was totally forgotten.

I stood next to the desk that held the telephones for public use with one of those two telephones smacked up against my ear. I hung onto the telephone receiver holding it up against my head afraid that I would miss a word, a sound, anything that would tell me that it wasn't my husband that was about to code.

"How long has this phone been off the hook?" I heard in the background.

"Don't know. Just hang it up. I'm sure whoever was on the other end has gotten tired of waiting by now."

"No, no, please, don't hang up," I shouted.

Then the line was dead. A few seconds later, the dial tone was blaring in my ear.

I was so angry I wanted to shout and scream but what I actually did was cry. That was what anger did to me. It made me cry.

I immediately redialed the CCU extension and listened to it ring and ring.

I dialed the phone a third time and it was answered.

"CCU, may I help you?"

"I'm Ellen Holcombe. May I see my husband?"

"I'll get his nurse. Hold on please," and she laid the phone down again.

I wanted to go running through both sets of double doors but I held myself back trying to maintain control over my thoughts and feelings.

Maybe I was wrong. Maybe it was someone else's name I heard.

No – no – I'm sure I heard Mr. Holcombe.

"This is Tammy, may I help you?" said a professional sounding voice.

"I'm Ellen Holcombe. I would like to see my husband."

"I'm sorry, Mrs. Holcombe, there are some people working with him now. If you will have a seat in the waiting room, we will call you and tell you to come back here to see him. It will be a few minutes," then the line was dead again.

I was allowed to ask no questions.

I slowly walked to the chairs where I fell down in physical and mental exhaustion. Angry tears were streaming down my face and I was sure a look of total hatred for anyone and anything daring to cross my path could be read in the lines etched in my brow.

I was alone. God, why am I always alone?

I worried and waited. That seemed to be how I spent all of my time lately. I must worry and wait and worry and wait.

The ring of the telephone suddenly filled the waiting area. None of the other people sitting on the chairs look as if they planned to answer the insistent noise.

I jumped up, ran across the room, and yanked the receiver up.

"Waiting Room," I whispered into the receiver.

"Mrs. Holcombe?"

"Yes."

"You need to come to your husband's room to speak to the Critical Care Specialist."

"Which room?"

"Six."

I walked, no, I ran through both sets of double doors and slowed my pace when I actually entered the CCU. I spotted room six where gowned and masked people were milling around Sonny's bed. He was totally out of it, unconscious, and the person nearest Sonny was barking out orders.

"Mrs. Holcombe, we need you to sign the form the nurse is holding over there so we perform a special procedure to get a line into your husband to begin dialysis if that becomes necessary."

My mouth was open and I was stunned to the point that I had no words.

"His kidneys have stopped functioning possibly due to the use of the blood thinning drug or perhaps an allergy to the dye used during the catherization. We're not sure what caused the problem at this moment. We need you to sign the form before we can proceed."

I thought those were the words of explanation that I heard. I was not sure of anything that I heard. All I know was that my husband looked like he was going to die.

Before I could get the ink to the paper, the critical care specialist said, "I can't get the needle into the artery. It will have to be done by a surgeon. The form won't be necessary for this procedure. We'll have to do it a different way."

I walked out of the room in a daze.

I walked to the nursing desk and gave the attendant my cell phone number. I needed to go to my car. I needed to be alone.

The night was long as I sat in the passenger seat of the car and tried to sleep. I needed to sleep so I wouldn't worry about what was happening with Sonny. Everything woke me up, from car headlights shining brightly to the slamming of the doors of each vehicle within listening distance.

At 4:00 a.m., I gathered my last set of clean clothes that I had with me and proceeded to enter the hospital in search of a restroom with a door that I could lock so I could clean up and feel a little more human before I started calling the CCU to check on Sonny.

After changing clothes, I returned to the car to deposit my dirty clothes before starting the long walk to the waiting room. As soon as I entered the waiting room, the telephone rang. I yanked it up.

"Mrs. Holcombe, please."

"Speaking."

"Your husband would like for you to come to his room."

I threw the phone onto the cradle and ran to the CCU.

I walked into the room to see my husband's eyes open as he watched me enter.

"Hi, Babe," he said as I smiled from ear to ear.

We chatted for a little while. He was not aware of anything that had happened. I would tell him a little at a time so he could absorb the fact that I was almost a widow, once again.

CHAPTER 23
THE OLD PEOPLE SMELL

"Sonny, I love you. I will always love and take care of you. Don't ever think that I won't. This is how I see our future, Sonny. This is the dream I had and I hope and pray that we will be able to grow old together and live like this…"

The house smelled of old people just the way our house used to smell twenty years earlier while my mother was still on this Earth. I didn't like the smell. It permeated the nostrils, stained my clothing with an odor that seemed like it would never come out, and followed me everywhere I went. No matter how much scrubbing and spraying and cleaning I would do, it was there.

What caused the old people smell? Of course, people will tell you it was unclean bodies, unclean clothes, and unclean general areas, but that was not true. The old people smell came with old people. I knew that for a fact. I was an old person.

I always swore I would never be like my mother who was not a clean person, but it seemed the smell had come with me anyway.

How do you get rid of it?

I didn't know except maybe die. I didn't like it and I was going to work on it and keep working on it until it disappeared, or I did. One or the other will happen.

I knew I cleaned every day. Of course, I can't clean like the twenty-year-old I used to be. I can't climb up on things and crawl under things but I did the best I could.

I had a little dog and I had a husband who was in chronically poor health and I had four cats roaming through my small world trying to keep us company. Neither the animals nor the husband were going to disappear any time soon. I didn't want them to. So, I guessed I was destined to have a house that smelled like old people. Anyone who visited would have to realize that was a fact.

In order to keep myself going and my husband, we tended to be the neighborhood watchers. Not officially. We were just home all of the time so we knew more about what was going on around us than anybody else in the neighborhood because they were out and about enjoying life at work, at school, and at play.

So, our thing was neighbor watching. We watched the comings and goings, the spats, and happiness that took place around us.

The neighbors on the right side of our house was a deaf couple. I often wished I had learned to sign when I was younger then I would be able to talk to them in a way that they would understand, especially now, since the young couple were expecting a baby. I couldn't really speak to them like I would really like to but I would make them something; a handmade, honorary grandmother gift to an infant. I hoped the baby didn't have the same affliction they did. If it did, it will get along just fine. They seemed to be doing very well in their silent world.

The lady on the left side has got to be pushing the age of ninety. She had health care workers wandering in and out and she had family members who dropped in on her at various times, usually the weekends or five o'clock and after on week days. I was not for sure if they were checking on her health or checking to see if she had died yet. They never seemed like very happy people. She seemed nicer than any of her family members who seemed to be a little put out by having to take care of her.

The lady on the left across the street from us had a teenage son who was built the size of a football player. He didn't play football. He was just a big, triple X sized boy who was still in high school. I believed that he and his mother were just about all each had.

The house almost directly across from us sat backwards to the street. It faced no road and the people would not stay in it very long whenever they rented the place.

It belonged to the church so I believed that whoever was in there had something to do with the church. I didn't know what and I didn't really care what. I never much cared for the preacher of that church who lived one house beyond the backwards house. He wasn't friendly or inviting. If he couldn't invite me to his church, then I didn't feel I needed to grace his presence with mine.

I didn't know, maybe it was the wrong way to be but it was the way I felt about it. He was not friendly, he was not outgoing, and he was not very caring because he had known through his flock that I had a great deal of trouble financially and medically with my husband who had nearly died four separate times within the last year. Not one word of sympathy or help was offered by him.

In our little island, in our home that Habitat built, we were growing old and we were neighborhood watching.

We watched the children walk by our house on the way to the public pool in the park about a half a mile from us. All colors, all races, all nationalities, we enjoyed the steady march.

The only time that I could recall that the police got involved with our lives, other than to give me a copy of a judgment for unpaid debt, was when the town police officer came knocking at the door wanting to know if Sonny had heard the disturbance.

Sonny opened the door slowly and the town police officer said, "Hi, I'm investigating a disturbance that occurred across the street between that house there, the white one with its back to you, and the preacher's house. It was up on the hill slightly. It happened last night around nine o'clock. We wanted to know if you heard or saw anything."

Sonny looked at him and replied, "I was out about nine o'clock walking the dog. I heard what sounded like a bunch of kids yelling and having a good time. I didn't pay any attention to them. There are a bunch of kids on this street. Not that they live on this street, but they are always hanging out on this street. The preacher has several children and they have friends. So I don't think anything of a bunch of kids yelling and having a good time."

The town officer continued, "You didn't see anybody?"

"No, I didn't see a soul," replied Sonny. "But like I said, I heard people. No one sounded like they were being hurt. You know how kids scream when someone's chasing them. That's what it sounded like. Why are you questioning me?"

"Well, someone said you were out walking your dog."

"Who said that?"

"Just some other people that we are questioning. So we wanted to know if you had seen anything."

"The person who told you I was walking my dog, do you think they were involved in this?"

"No, he is just a person of interest we were questioning. Nothing specific. No specific charges have been made against anybody yet."

"What kind of disturbance was it?"

"It was domestic. If not domestic, it was an assault."

"Did someone get hurt?"

"Yes, the victim is in the hospital."

"Is it bad?"

"Bad enough."

"Should I be worried about anybody seeing me?"

"No, I wouldn't worry. It's nothing really. I believe it's just a domestic disturbance. So you just need to keep your eyes open."

"Keep my eyes open for what?"

"Just keep your eyes open for strangers. And call us if anything at all happens or if you hear anybody around your house."

I was standing behind my husband and I heard this entire conversation. It was time for me to chime in.

"If it's nothing, why are you warning us?"

"Ma'am, we're just trying to be careful and cover all of the bases. We don't think anything is going to happen. We don't think it was anything other than a domestic disturbance. But, we don't know yet. It's time for me to leave. If you can think of anything that might help us try to determine what happened, give me a call. I'm Officer Martin and you can reach me at the town hall."

"Thank you, Sir. We appreciate your watching over us all."

He walked down the sidewalk and away leaving a trail of mystery and worry behind him.

"Sonny, did you see anybody?"

"No, Ellen, I didn't see anybody."

"But you did hear the screams."

"Yeah. They sounded like they were kids playing. That's what I told the officer."

"Is that what you think it was?"

"He doesn't seem to think it was. I guess maybe it might be a problem. What are we supposed to do now?"

"What we always do, hide and watch, just hide and watch."

Nothing came of the threat that my husband and I felt. We were grateful.

That's how I wanted us to live the remainder of our days. I wanted us to be together and I wanted to hide and watch the young people as we grew old in the company of each other.

I never told Sonny about the carjacking. I mentioned it only as a dream just in case I had a slip of the tongue. I didn't want him to worry about my stubborn need and desire to sleep in the car. I never told him that I needed the comfort of something familiar surrounding me in its cocoon of protection. My car was the closest thing to a home that I could find when I was in that parking garage away from my beloved Stillwell.

Approximately four weeks after the insertion of the twenty-sixth stent in his heart, Sonny was released from the hospital and I drove him to our home in Stillwell, the first Habitat House in our County, our little white house with black shutters.

This is where we will live as long as we have each other.

CHAPTER 24
PEOPLE WATCHING

I was doing it again. I was people watching in a popular cafeteria where there seemed to be a constant flow of bodies in and out as they hurried on to meet the demands of their busy lives.

An elderly couple with the gentleman riding a wheelchair seemed to be the happiest of those sitting at tables within my sight line.

The gentleman, I will call him John, was wearing an oxygen hose on his face to enhance his ability to breathe the good warm air filled with food smells that were caused by the cooking of the fine cuisine for which the restaurant was famous.

The little gray-haired lady, I will call Mary, made sure everything that John wanted to eat was within his reach. She did not baby John at all, but she made life a little easier for the disabled man.

Mary kept a good stream of conversation going using a pleasant, calm voice at all times.

When she finished her meal, she sat at the table and patiently waited for her companion, John, to place his eating utensils on the plate and reach for his cup of decaf coffee.

She talked to him and he answered with short sentences or one word. She looked at him with old eyes displaying a love of many years.

Mary, a petite lady, of about five feet or less, gathered up everything and started pushing the John filled wheelchair to the exit.

I jumped up to open the door to allow them to leave without the struggle that would have occurred without my assistance. It made my heart feel good to help.

This cafeteria seemed to be the place for family and friends. They outnumbered the solitary diners much to my chagrin because on many occasions since the passing of my husband, I was a solitary diner not by choice.

I also saw the servers who had not been called upon to take care of people at the tables rush to decorate the interior of the restaurant with Santas, snowmen, and poinsettias to highlight the coming holiday season. In no time at all, they had created a Christmas atmosphere filled with laughter and joy.

Joy was hard for me this year. Sonny, my beloved husband, companion, travel mate, and best friend, succumbed to a life-ending colonoscopy three weeks before Thanksgiving, one day before my sixtieth birthday, and less than two months before the upcoming Christmas holiday.

I was sitting behind a table filled with the books I was trying to sell in order to meet the obligations incurred while trying to keep my husband alive.

I struggled to force a smile on my face to overcome the black, empty feeling that filled my heart.

I was trying so hard not to think about my reasons for sadness, but Sonny would never, ever leave my thoughts.

My eyes were tearing up again. I had to force my thoughts away from my Sonny and how much I missed him.

I saw a single soul sitting at a table on my left side. I will call the man Jim. He appeared to be a gruff individual with a no nonsense attitude. He wasn't wearing a wedding band, but with men it wasn't unusual for the absence of a band, and still have a wonderful wife sitting at home.

He must have asked to speak to the cafeteria manager. He drummed his fingers from both hands on the table as he looked irritated and unhappy.

"He is busy right at this moment, but he will be out to speak with you in a few minutes," explained a noticeably nervous server.

"That's all right," said Jim to the busy waitress. "If he is too busy to talk to me, I understand."

"Sir, if you can wait, he will be out to talk to you."

"I'm busy too. I'm eating right now so I'm not going anywhere."

He continued to eat stopping every so often to drum his fingers and look gruff.

"He is still busy, but he will be here to speak with you," whispered the worried waitress.

He could see the worry on her face and he reached out to her grabbing at her arm, "Don't worry, Honey, it's not about you.

You could see the tension melt from the waitress with those words.

Jim continued to eat and drum his fingers. When he finished his meal he sat and waited and drummed his fingers.

"Do you know the manager's name?" he asked the same harried waitress.

"Yes, Sir, his name is Donald Androsian."

"Can you spell that last name for me?"

"A-N-D-R-O-S-I-A-N," she said distinctly so Jim could write it down on the small piece of paper he was holding.

"Where is your main office?"

"Alabama."

"Do you have that address?"

"No, Sir, but the lady at the cash register may have it."

He stood up and started to put on his coat. He had to pause to let diners carrying food-filled trays pass.

He saw me watching him.

"Busy corner here," he said in a booming voice.

"Yes, it is. It's kind of dangerous to cross the oncoming traffic," I said with a smile.

He crossed the aisle and stood in front of my table filled with books.

"I'm a local author. I have a book of Christmas stories you need to buy for your wife or girlfriend."

"I wish I had one," Jim said as he shrugged his shoulders and walked away.

He stopped at the cash register near the exit door to pay for his meal and said a little too loudly, "Do you have the address for the main office in Alabama?"

"No, Sir, but you can find it on the internet."

"Thank you, Young Lady," he said and finally left after having stirred up several employees with what everyone believed to be a complaint. He never did get to speak to the manager who was extremely busy with all of the extra holiday traffic being served in his cafeteria.

I was sure the home office would get the complaint, whatever it was. Jim appeared to be a man who, like a dog with a bone, would chew away at something until he felt relieved or too tired to continue chewing.

It was mid-afternoon and the traffic pattern was beginning to slow. It wouldn't last long because the evening meal rush would rev up momentarily.

I hadn't had much success at selling my books, only two had been purchased but I considered it a winning experience if I sold just one. Two book sales made it a double win.

The pause gave me time to reflect upon the nice young men I encountered when I made my trips to my parked car to retrieve my selling materials.

The first young man of what appeared to be Asian descent stood with the door handle in his hand waiting for me to get closer before he yanked the heavy glass and metal door. The show of respect floored me, especially coming from a young man I did not know.

As I exited the mall to get my second load of books, another young college age man held the door for me. I smiled warmly and nodded to acknowledge his kindness.

It didn't take a lot to impress me. Both of those young men were appreciated by this little old lady.

While I was contemplating the unexpected signs of respect, my small book selling table became surrounded by people looking at the pictures in the collage I prepared to spark interest in my mystery novel.

I guessed it was a good idea. I had one of those every once in a while; a good idea, I meant.

Two more books were purchased bringing me to a total so far of four out the door.

The cafeteria was full of people who needed to complete their chores and not waste time with an old lady trying to foist her novels onto unsuspecting victims.

I was beginning to feel better about being here until I was told that it was snowing outside and the roads were getting hard to manage.

I had to wait and worry about what the roads would be like when I left here after four more hours.

Another lull but not before two more of precious volumes of words were sold.

It was usually a terrific book signing if I could sell ten books. I was well on my way to terrific.

The booths and tables were filling up again. Now, the all-day shoppers were tired and hungry. The new arrivals were anxious about getting the eating out of the way so they could go explore the Christmas wonders for sale throughout the mall.

I was tired of sitting behind this table. I got up and stretched my legs. A trip to the ladies' room was the only exercise I would be getting until I hit the magic hour of eight o'clock when I could pack up and drive for an hour and a half to my home in Stillwell. Hopefully, it would only take me that long, ninety minutes, but the falling snow may prolong the long, lonely drive.

Another book was purchased and this time it was by a man. He actually bought one of the anthologies that I was prone to giving away when someone buys two of my novels. It served as an added incentive, a simple come-on that worked once in a while.

Another book gone; this time it was my first novel. The total was now at eight. I was keeping my fingers crossed. I had about two more hours to reach the magic number of ten.

The looky-loos had appeared at the table several times today. Most told me "I don't have time to read" which in a few cases may have been true, but most of the time it was just a dishonest way of telling me they were not interested or they don't have the money. I would rather hear the truth.

I looked at the live poinsettias that had been placed on the half wall partition that separated this large room into two sections. Those deep red leaves remind me of my mother and her love for the Christmas plant.

Mom didn't inspire too many good memories because of the way she was acting a few years prior to her death. Old age made her mean and ugly when dealing with me. That attitude was the opposite of the mom who raised me.

It was nice to have a good memory about her love for poinsettias.

A lady sitting at the table directly in front of me was chatting with a woman who looked to be her mother. There was a strong facial resemblance.

236

The younger woman, I will call her Jill, was blessed with a beautiful face. She had a quiet, subtle beauty that radiated from her.

"I hope you weren't embarrassed with my stares," I said as she began to walk toward the exit. "I think you are so very pretty," I added in explanation.

"Thank you," was her humble reply.

She looked at my books questioning me about each volume. She chose two and I gave her the third, an anthology that contained my prize-winning short story.

My total now was ten sold and one given free. I had a terrific book signing with the possibility of selling even more.

"Do you like to read?"

"No, I wish I did," mumbled a lady as she past my table.

Again, I asked, "Do you like to read?" and a different lady stopped to look and decided to buy the small volume of Christmas stories.

One more hour needed to pass so I could go out and brave the winter storm during my long drive home.

A nice lady named Linda quizzed me about my writings. She purchased a book and went on her merry way.

That purchase had exceeded all of my expectations and made the long drive ahead of me a little more bearable.

Now the area in front of me was thinning out and I saw two older males sitting in different booths that were eating their suppers alone. Both had hair that was mostly white and thinning in spots. Both were nicely attired in clean casual clothes. Neither of them had a wedding band and the lack of a smile on either face told me they spent most of their days and nights alone.

I was sure Christmas held the same appeal for them as it did for me. Being alone did not allow for the feeling of great joy.

All of the late diners were arriving to eat before they headed for home and hearth.

Suddenly, the two diners were lonely no more and every booth and table seemed to be filling up rapidly. The older of the lonely men departed wearing a scowl across his handsome face.

"Have a good evening," I whispered as he passed my table.

"You, too, Lady," he told me as he continued to walk to the counter to pay for his food.

You can tell who the frequent visitors were to this eating establishment. After the meal had been consumed, they stacked the individual serving dishes in the same manner that the servers did when they were bussing the tables.

The second lonely man did just that. He stacked all of his serving dishes before he departed the table without leaving a tip. I was sure the stacking was helpful to the servers but "no tip" was not kind.

I arrived here at eleven o'clock in the morning and it was almost eight o'clock at night. It had been a long day but a terrific one.

I missed Sonny.

OTHER BOOKS WRITTEN BY LINDA HUDSON HOAGLAND:

FICTION

ONWARD & UPWARD

MISSING SAMMY

AN UNJUST COURT

SNOOPING CAN BE HELPFUL - SOMETIMES

SNOOPING CAN BE DOGGONE DEADLY

SNOOPING CAN BE DEVIOUS

SNOOPING CAN BE CONTAGIOUS

SNOOPING CAN BE DANGEROUS

THE BEST DARN SECRET

CROOKED ROAD STALKER

DEATH BY COMPUTER

THE BACKWARDS HOUSE

AN AWFULLY LONELY PLACE

NONFICTION

90 YEARS AND STILL GOING STRONG

QUILTED MEMORIES

LIVING LIFE FOR OTHERS

JUST A COUNTRY BOY: DON DUNFORD (Edited)

WATCH OUT FOR EDDY

THE LITTLE OLD LADY NEXT DOOR

COLLECTIONS

I AM… LINDA ELLEN (POETRY)

A COLLECTION OF WINNERS (SHORT PROSE)

55227159R00133

Made in the USA
Columbia, SC
15 April 2019